MY HEART BEATS FAST

Global Black Writers in Translation

Vanessa K. Valdés, Annette Joseph-Gabriel, and Nathan H. Dize, series editors

Global Black Writers in Translation publishes texts that explore the full spectrum of Black life and expression by authors of African descent, translated from their source languages into English. The series introduces anglophone readers to the range and complexity of Black literary and cultural production, history, and political thought, expanding existing literary canons and stretching them beyond their current national, geographic, and linguistic limits to foreground global diasporic Black writers, while also increasing the number of Black translators. Although expansive in geographic and temporal scope, what unifies the varied texts is their centering of Black experiences.

TITLES IN THIS SERIES:

Camille's Lakou, by Marie Léticée, translated by Kevin Meehan and Marie Léticée

Workshop of Silence / Atelier du silence, by Jean D'Amérique, translated by Conor Bracken

my heart beats fast

A NOVEL

NADIA CHONVILLE

Translated by Corine Labridy

Vanderbilt University Press
Nashville, Tennessee

Published 2026 by Vanderbilt University Press.
This edition is published by arrangement with Memoire d'encrier in conjunction with its duly appointed agents Books and More Agency #BAM, Paris, Frame, and 2 Seas Literary Agency Inc.

Library of Congress Cataloging-in-Publication Data on file

LCCN 2025037903
ISBN 978-0-8265-0821-8 (Paperback)
ISBN 978-0-8265-0822-5 (Hardcover)
ISBN 978-0-8265-0823-2 (ePub)
ISBN 978-0-8265-0824-9 (PDF)

Front cover image: Painting by agsandrew; Silhouette by Shiraufa

For Afef

Contents

Translator's Note, or, A Primer on Twenty-First-Century Antillean Grammars ix

THE ORANGE GROVE

To Lose Your Memory 5
To Avenge the Rootstock 10
To Hush the Frogs Now 17
To Return Under the Mango Tree 22
To Kill Dread 27
To Satisfy the *Makrels* 30
To Be on Television 33
To Enter the Sanctuary 37
To Snuff Out the Morning Light 42
To Be a Monster 45
To Live Free or Die 47
To Kill the Child Who Did Nothing 57

RÉGALE

To Inherit a Legacy 63
To Summon a Hurricane 70
To Return from Exile 73
To Make Maman Proud 79
To Burn the Trash 86
To Reveal the Trickery 88
To Offend the Church Roaches 92
To Bring Our Story to a Close 95

FOYAL

To Put an End to the Indivision 101
To Blow Everything Up 106
To Stop the Noise 112

To Break the Circle 118
To Make People Talk 124
To Erase His Face 127
To Honor the Wife 132
To Get Revenge 135
To Crush Our Silences 139
To Reopen a Tomb 143
To Know 145
To Not Know 150

Translator's Notes *155*

Translator's Note, or, A Primer on Twenty-First-Century Antillean Grammars

HOLD ON TIGHT. This is the story of a young man's vertiginous fall into madness and violence. And this is the story of the sister, mother, and foremothers who seek to understand what led him to murder. And this is the story of the ancestor whose century-long thirst for revenge spurred him on. And this is also the story of an island exhausted by neocolonialism and ravenous capitalism. Nadia Chonville layers these stories upon the greater history of Martinique with unflinching rigor and poetry, and with a grammar singularly fit for the times.

And what are these times? In the year following the publication of *Mon cœur bat vite*, in 2023, Martinique became the theater of bitter demonstrations against the unbearably high cost of living, which left several dead or injured. It is this anger, this frustration bubbling under the surface that Chonville sensed and captured in her novel. What might a grammar of senseless violence look like?

Jarring, rebellious, and complex to be sure. But Chonville writes violence with no complacency. She wants her readers to see it in its rawest form, but above all, she wants them to imagine a world after it, without it, and beyond it. The present translation stays as close as possible to that impossible grammar so as to reproduce its sense of urgency, its desire to urge us to look for other ways, lest we too succumb to madness, like Kim.

Madness is an orientation of the senses many of us are unfamiliar with. Stepping into Kim's madness means entering a space of confusion and discomfort. The challenge as a translator was to let this madness speak for itself without attempting to scrub it clean, to make it more legible or palatable in English, to smooth its jagged edges. Madness owes us neither transparency nor ease. As Kim comes undone, his thoughts meander, his sentences lengthen, and punctuation falters, leaving him (and the reader) breathless. I remained as faithful as possible to Chonville's grammar of madness and changed the punctuation only when absolutely necessary.

But madness isn't the only loquacious presence in *My Heart Beats Fast*. The island, too, speaks through Kim's voice, through his sister Édith's voice, through their foremothers and aunties, related or not, through the nosy neighbors and the bigoted gossips, and through an omnipresent chorus of nonhuman existences. The island has its own lexicon and its own grammar. When it speaks through its inhabitants, sometimes it erupts in bursts of Kreyol, sometimes in French, and sometimes in a beautifully chaotic mix of the two. In most cases, I followed Chonville's cue and left much of the Kreyol untranslated (unless it contained an important clue, in which case, I provided a translator's note)—readers will have to trust that she left them enough context not to feel completely lost but should know that sometimes she didn't. A reasonable dose of bewilderment can be a humbling experience, and at its most magical degree, it can even offer a natural high. In rarer cases, to reproduce the feeling of languages clashing, a characteristic of Antillean literature that is always at risk of being effaced in translation, I follow the example of Linda Coverdale, one of Patrick Chamoiseau's stellar cadre of translators, and attach an English word to a French or Kreyol one—for instance, *marraine*-godmother, or *maré tèt*-headscarf.

Translators of the French-writing Antilles know this: the words *case*, *morne*, and *l'en-ville* pose thick challenges. *Case* is the French spelling of the word for a Creole home. It is not exactly a *cabin*, nor is it a *hut* or a *shack*, for a *case* can be big or small, run down or glammed up, ancient or flirting with modernity, lonely and nestled on the volcano's slope or cramped in the city amid other *cases*. Untranslated and italicized, the word *case* ran the risk of sounding like something else to the ear of an Anglophone reader's mind. To avoid confusion and to double down on the text's Kreyoleness, I opted for the Kreyol spelling of the word: *kaz*. While *kaz* is admittedly more used in the neighboring sister island of Guadeloupe, it pops up occasionally in Martinican Kreyol and offers a sonic and visual middle ground between the French *case* and the Martinican *kay*.

The *morne* is a beloved fixture of the Antillean topography, a round hill that has long cradled the people's misery and concealed their rebellions (Aimé Césaire showed us how in *Cahier d'un retour au pays natal*). I chose to leave this natural monument untouched.

L'en-ville, meaning in the most literal sense *the in-city*, is a proteiform concept that is currently in flux. The Martinican art journal *Zist* dedicated its twenty-seventh volume (2024) to it, theorizing it under its Kreyol spelling: *lanvil*. "*Lanvil*," writes Afro-futurist author Michael Roch, "and not any other term, because from now on, our humanity—wherever it is—cannot do without the catastrophic force that is urbanity. Our past, present and future inhabitants are urban, that is, constantly connected to large human concentrations."[1] Chonville herself penned a poem in that issue, in which she too uses the spelling *lanvil.*[2] For this reason, I adopted the latter spelling in this translation, presenting *l'en-ville* alternatively as *lanvil*-downtown, or simply *lanvil.*

Never not vexing, the words *Nègre* and *Négresse* remain recalcitrant to translation. Not quite the N-word, nor Negro nor Black, they are impossibly French-Antillean. They tell exactly the story of the forced encounter between French thought and Black bodies, and they rehearse its ache. As René Ménil sharply put it: "Ce n'est pas parce qu'ils sont nègres que les Africains et les Antillais ont été colonisés, c'est au contraire parce qu'ils ont été colonisés . . . que, noirs, ils sont devenus des nègres (avec toutes les connotations qui ont servi aux Blancs à constituer ce concept au cours de leur pratique coloniale)." (It is not because they are *Nègres* that Africans and Antilleans were colonized, on the contrary, it is because they were colonized, that from Black they became *Nègres* [with all the connotations White people mobilized to constitute this concept all throughout their colonial practice].)[3] Here again, I chose not to translate, to sit with this untranslatability and this fluidity, too, and to accept them as constitutive of an Antillean history that is still being written.

Finally, a note on gender. Chonville is a staunch Black feminist, well-known in Martinique for her public interventions against feminicide and domestic violence. Black feminism, as Afro-American scholar bell hooks defines it, "is a movement to end sexism, sexist exploitation, and oppression," for all those who suffer under their yoke—women *and* men, cis or trans.[4] This all-encompassing emancipation project is particularly necessary in the Antilles, a region that has historically been misogynistic and transphobic. Although they have always enriched the fabric of Antillean society, queer lives have often been ignored or even, at times, derided in Antillean literature. Chonville is a member of a promising new cohort of Antillean authors who have been especially attentive to writing sensitive, rich, layered, and all-in-all ordinary portrayals of LGBTQ lives. While Kim is a young trans man, in *My Heart Beats Fast,* his gender is neither spectacular nor is it the reason why he commits the violent acts that propel the story. Rather, by following Kim from childhood to manhood, Chonville gets at what it is like to experience growing up socialized as a girl in Martinique, a time as fraught with danger as it is steeped with nostalgia, and what it is like to be a disenfranchised young Black man on an island that struggles to recognize the afterlives of colonialism in the ongoing capitalist schema. At the same time, she doesn't shy from exposing the transphobic side of Martinican society, reproducing the terrible grammar of misgendering. To balance this, she also shows what acceptance and love can look like. If Édith cannot condone Kim's violence, she never doubted in her heart that he was her little brother all along. I carefully follow Chonville's steps as she guides the reader through the changing ways with which Kim and others understand his gender over the course of the story.

It is an exciting and precious time for Antillean literature. Chonville's grave and poetic writing is emblematic of a new generation of authors who shatter taboos and proclaim their commitment to freedom in literature. It has been my aim to share this sense of excitement and experimentation with an English-speaking readership.

Notes

1. Michael Roch, "L'Appel de Lanvil," *Zist,* no. 27 (December 2024), 5.
2. Nadia Chonville, "Soukounian," *Zist,* no. 27 (December 2024), 50.
3. René Ménil, "Le spectre de Gobineau," *Antilles déjà Jadis précédé de Tracées* (Jean-Michel Place, 1999), 97. Italics in the original.
4. bell hooks, *Feminism Is for Everybody* (South End Press, 2000), viii.

my
heart
beats
fast

The Orange Grove

Listen in the wind
For the sobbing bush,
It's the breath of the ancestors.

"THE BREATHS," BIRAGO DIOP, *LEURRES ET LUEURS*
(1960, éd. Présence Africaine; translation by Corine Labridy)

To Lose Your Memory

FIRST, KIM CARESSES THE BOTTLE. His endless fingers trace the straight, angular body of the tempered glass where the raw gold awaits. His black eyes probe the liquid's depths and rob the angels of their due. His thumb pops the top. His hand firmly seizes the bottle's body and pours its incandescent waters into a cold glass. At long last, the sun-filled cascade sweeps away Kim's pain, his fever, his heart adrift, and in the bewitching music of the alcohol and the ice, his memory courts the abyss. He breathes, and an hour stretches between his nares without sound nor sigh. Remains only the chiseled clamor of the passing time and the commandments the rum murmurs in his ear.

The alcohol tells him: Kim, make me dance. Lull me in the generous folds of your palms. Bring to my waters the dark fleshiness of your quivering lips and your ample nostrils, and close your eyes. Kim ebbs his eyelids and the alcohol tells him: let us soar together to the zeniths of your errantries. I will bring you back to the green slopes of the *morne*, the hill where it all began. We will awaken the silence you buried there. Together, let us dig up the flanks of this *morne* that dominates the sea and the ocean from its impetuous height. Plunge your hands into your mothers' soil, just where the damp odor of the blood shed in the humus stretches the cries of the martyrs into infinite sighs.

Kim's glass is empty, but the rum is still talking, and the night goes on whispering its melancholic chant without ever offering him another glass.

A little. That's how much my brother always drank, and he'd do so to the soundtrack of all the voices of all the women who imparted us good manners since the cradle. They held the entire world on their crowned heads of *manman*-mothers, yet their words deluged nothing but decrees for sacrifice and patience. And that was their grand scheme for little girls like us. Kim and I suckled on their saintly words: we were very obedient daughters. Maman beamed with pride in front of everyone she knew. A girl must behave, that's the least she can do. *Sé sa yo di*, yes, that's what they'd say, and me with my head in my books, and Kim in his permanent reverie, we didn't misbehave, and we didn't throw fits. The mere thought of Maman's anger snuffed out our mischief, and Kim, secretly, from what I know, hoped to be one day rewarded for good behavior. When the house was sound asleep, Kim would slip out from under his sheets, fall to his knees in front of his bed and pray to a rather disparate cast of saints and *loas*-spirits that he might one day be recognized for the boy he'd always been and the man he'd become. While feverishly waiting for that day to come and as a humble penance, Kim never asked for more than he was given. He murdered in his belly the desire to ask for seconds and to lick the batter out of the cake pan with abandon. And when Maman covered her little girl with kisses and smiles, Kim consented to the lie to make his mother happy and to one day deserve the body he saw when he closed his eyes.

From these ascetic days, Kim conserved a legendary moderation. He has never been drunk. He has never lost his mind. But not that night. That night, Kim taunts the child buried in his memory and dies in a glass of alcohol. He drinks, he drinks too much. He offers his head to the *makrels*, those neighborhood gossips safe behind their blinds who have made it their life's work to legislate girlhood with frills, prohibitions, and impeccable French grammar. Kim drinks. On the bar top of a rum hole in *Foyal*-Fort-de-France, he makes his glass spin-spin-spin, he no longer sees straight, he sings and sways on his stool, extending the elongated curve of his limbs to the shudders of his companions of trance.

And when in the heart of the tropical night he gets up and hits the curb, he walks, gets lost, and drowns his drunken eye in the moon's steel. Trouble is, he is not drunk enough to forget the eyes of the one he killed.

That's how I imagine my brother lived his last hours of freedom. That's how he tried to disappear, five years ago, in the one-too-many drink. The ethyl drug gnawed at his muscles, dissolved his armor, but not his crime. And when the police found and shackled my brother, he no longer had the straight spine of a warrior. There was no pride in his last glance. He was just a lost boy, astray in his own convictions, imploring me, between bated sobs, to forgive him.

I forgive nothing.

Tomorrow begins Kim's trial for murder. Kim refuses to plead guilty. To survive, I believe, he convinced himself he was a hero. Yet it's not an exceptional act that landed him in jail. Killing is not that hard. It's a banal gesture. Millions of animals are slaughtered every day to feed voracious BBQs where no one can tell the lamb from the beef and the turkey from the chicken. Every year for Easter, hordes of crabs are massacred on the beach by sadistic knives, for the pleasure of slurp-slurping the fragrant Colombo sauce from their carapace. And for Christmas, we used to sacrifice pigs right here in the *lakou*, but today, who knows on what continent died the pigs we consume? We are carnivorous creatures. Killing is a simple gesture we pay no mind to. It's what comes next, the terror. The dizzying silence, when the soul escapes, slipping through your body. The intense silence in the body of the murderer slowly reborn. The silence of a heart that no longer beats, a heart for which love, in the blink of an eye, has become a foreign land.

I could also kill. I could kill my brother. I could kill the murderer who robbed me of my suns, my sleep, my memory, and my blood. I could, too, become a monster of silence. But my life would amount to no more than a long despair.

I hesitated a long time before coming here. I hesitated a long time before confronting this memory because I wanted to survive it. It was easier to let a forgetting settle in, and no one, no, no one should have the right to dictate the time and place of my rage. But tomorrow leaves me with no choice. I will have to take the stand and tell the tale of this bloody day as if I had lived it. I will have to answer the questions that are on everyone's lips. I will have to let my anger erupt at last.

So here I am, now, in this *kaz*, this Creole home, alone and resigned. Five years of investigation and instruction have covered the tiled floor with a powdery coat. My bare feet leave their prints behind. Unsettled, the dust sketches spirals in the air where the last rays of the day's sun come to play. I could linger and watch the night slowly devour this suspended abode and linger some more. But my skin itches now, it buzzes with impatience, impatient to dive into the floor of this *kaz*, to melt in its walls. My body is ready to cross over, and I, too, am ready.

To relive the day when my whole world capsized, I painted a drawing of my ancestor Ayo on the living room wall. It is an ancient vévé. It's a vaudou symbol that traces the edge of the land of the dead and the contours of the world of the living. I mixed the ink of my own blood with fava bean powder to paint this sign on the walls of this tortured home, and here I am, Breaths, at your door. I am Édith, heir to the priestess Ayo. I inherited from my mothers the protection of Oshun and the volcano Hairun. I am powerful enough, and I fear nothing. No wound can kill a woman twice dead. Let me enter this wall and its secrets. I want to know what happened here, in this *kaz*. I want to know each word each gesture each feeling my brother sweat here, five years ago. I want to know why he murdered my child.

To Avenge the Rootstock

IT'S A CREOLE HOME. A *kaz.*

It's a Creole home clinging onto the side of a verdant *morne* in the kingdom where, at night, frogs sing their own epics.

It's a Creole home, a *kaz.* It's still a Creole home, a *kaz,* even though roof tiles made of clay have replaced sheets of corrugated iron, and even though pink marble tops on coffee tables have smoothed out the indignity of humanity. It's a Creole home, a *kaz.* Because a *Nègre,* black as night, was born here to die, it's a *kaz* made of compacted mud where the kitchen provides no more heat than strictly necessary to feed him the pittance that will keep him working. It's a *kaz* fit for a petty bourgeois who puffs his chest because he bought an Audi on credit. It's a burnt sienna *kaz,* dropped at the edge of the asphalt, with an electric gate, swimming pool, and vegetable garden. An honest *kaz.* Eco-friendly, too. The sun heats the water. The water is then treated-gobbled by hungry bacteria that eat the *Nègre*'s shit and turn it into fertile silt. Pressed against the flank of a well-behaved *morne,* it's a *kaz,* an Antillean home, shaded by the menacing branches of a kapok tree where three *Négresses* remained hung by the neck for two long months, to serve as an example, many moons ago. That's where Kim, dragged to the edge of the abyss by a liquid rage, took refuge five years ago, on a clear April night.

In the wall, I am no more than a mist of senses, and I see him. He is a handsome young man. His brow is smooth, and not a single white hair illuminates his braids, but the flight has bent his back. It is astonishing how drunks always find their way back to an asylum that will shelter their blues. After a long peregrination, Kim sets foot on the large veranda of this *kaz* at the hour when the stars still quarrel with the dew, and he enters the sleepy domain through the main door. The place is spacious, comfortable. This secluded *kaz* made of wood reminds him a little bit of Maman's home. The white tiled floor, the large shutters opened to the coolness of the tree-filled veranda bring him back to those mornings when he would watch her sway softly in the doorway. The light would paint lines on Maman's skin while her eyes gazed vaguely at the garden. It was the same red shutters, with slats so warped that no one ever bothers trying to close them. Except on hurricane days. Massive dark old-fashioned pieces of furniture, left behind by one ancestor or another, invade the living room. Impossible to get rid of those relics. Impossible to throw them away because they are still in good shape. Impossible to give them away because they are too heavy. Impossible to burn them: this wood doesn't burn. "And you can't sell them. It's too old to be elegant. Not enough to be vintage," Kim tells his hostage, who stares at him from a green leather couch, belly exposed, disheveled by a night cut short, and listens, petrified, to the logorrhea of the love-starved being who has entered his home at 3:00 A.M.: "*Ou ka santi an lanvi brilé yo, di mwen,* you'd gladly burn these old things, wouldn't you? To not see them anymore. To not have to talk about them anymore. Admit it, we're all like that here. I won't tell the ghosts. I'm not judging. Everybody keeps their old things until they become so ingrained that they no longer see them. Me, I will never get rid of the musty wood of Maman's wardrobes. Never. This smell, do you smell it? It's Maman. Her soul, her blood. You cannot get rid of blood, you cannot get rid of its stain. It's a body that doesn't die. The taste of iron on my tongue, is it the blood of your mother? Is that it? It's everywhere. I breathe it, the walls are painted with it. She is there, look! There! By your grand mahogany shutters, is that her? Is that her standing straight as an arrow in the shadow? Looking down on you, without a word? Is that her, that black reflection that thrones well above you? Your mother is a queen. She holds onto her throne with an iron grip. These tears, here, on the armrest, were carved by her nails, I am sure of it. And her fingers polished this wood, and it is still here. She is still here, too. I feel those things. I feel your mother's presence when I rock back and forth in this chair. They don't make rocking chairs like they used to. At those new furniture stores, you can buy the same one for five hundred bucks, and in one year, it will wobble, and in two, you'll have to chuck it. I think I'll stay here for a bit. By your window. With your mother. You don't mind, do you? Of course, you don't."

Kim's long legs have run their last marathon. They can carry him no more. He collapses in the rocking chair, and with a sorrowful groan, he exhales all the excess his body had held onto for the flight. Here he is, now adrift in a destiny that has just one destination. His crime echoes against the walls, and his cold eye cannot hide the panic that grips him. Kim sways, astray, while under the extinguished suns, the slumber of some strangles the cries of others. Dread crawls like a *milpat*, a beast with a thousand legs, across the tiles. It zig-zig-zag-zags from one end of the living room to the other and writhes with joy at the sight of the criminal's naked foot on the floor. So the vile gluttonous beast slithers the long liana that is its body toward him, across the washed-out sandstone. Between its fangs, a deadly silence. On this sprawling floor, the world dwells breathlessly. Daylight treads in, and dread swoops in for the kill.

Kim springs up. "Fucking hell, I'm thirsty. I need water. Don't move, Laurent, I have my eye on you. Bottled water. That's all I drink. I don't trust tap water. You can't trust anybody here. Ah, you keep water in the fridge. That's good. Water, lime. Dry. I'll need nothing else until dawn. *Ou ni sitwon, hen?* Didn't I see a potted lime tree on the veranda? I will purge some of its juice into my glass. I'll take a branch if you don't mind. This poor tortured tree in its pot, it will do it some good to be trimmed a bit."

Kim leaves his glass on the windowsill and steps onto the veranda. The knife in his hand drips with blood. I am not the only one bearing witness to Kim's acts from the in-between-worlds. An ancestor is there too, who slips out of the shadow to put her diaphanous hand on the neglected glass. Kim zigs and zags on the veranda and hums a song that the ancestor recognizes. It's a song that speaks of her home. She wrote it. Her tenebrous shadow stretches against the opposite wall, and I discover her face and her name. It's Ayo, the first among us to have set foot on Martinique's soil in 1812. Yes, I recognize her. How could I forget this face, round and proud, that began haunting me five Lents ago? With her long eyes fixated on her descendant, the ghost of Ayo clasps the edge of the shutter with her charcoal hands, observes Kim on the veranda clumsily rummaging through the branches of the old lime tree, and she trembles. And with her, the whole house begins to tremble.

"We used to have a lime tree, too," Kim tells Laurent. With a push of his foot, the rocking chair resumes its slow dance. "That lime tree is my oldest memory of home. I still have its scent right here, in the palm of my hands. I remember its flowers. And I remember . . .

Ugh, your limes are dry! Where did you get your seedling? These are dusty wild limes. No one ever taught you how to graft a lime tree? You should have bought a grafted one! What do you make with this besides *ti-punch*? Loser. Anyway. Maman, she had a real lime tree, a grafted one. Its limes were as big as oranges, and the zest . . . Its fragrance lingered on your hand all day if you picked one in the morning. Limes aren't about tang at all, they're about fragrance. A real lime isn't sour, it's a caress. I'll press some of these leaves into my water, that'll give it more aroma than this sorry skeleton of a lime. It will be just like a *madou*.[1] That's all it's good for, your wild lime tree. Mmmm, now that's a quality brew, dayum! Oh come now, don't be sore. Sing with me instead. *Siwo! Ban mwen an nonm dous kon siwo! Madou siwo . . .*"

With each sip, Kim sinks deeper into our oldest memory. He tells it to his hostage: he loves to tell this story. That day, at Maman's, Kim was running across the grass, but he wasn't very sturdy on his legs yet. I was chasing him, and Kim was squeaking with glee as he fled with his arms spread like airplane wings. And when I would get too close, Kim would close his eyes. That's how he fell against the lime tree, I think. But Kim always had his own version of the story: "The tree was still young," he tells his host. "But you should have seen its motherfucking thorns! They tore into my skin, my arms, my back. I remember the dress I was wearing that day. A gift from my godmother. It was torn to shreds. But I couldn't care less. I hated that dress anyway. I don't blame the lime tree. It took revenge on me for what it suffered as a sapling. I'm telling you. It was revenge. There is no doubt. It was a strong tree at birth. It was a rootstock. Its race had crossed centuries continents pandemics hurricanes, and it still stood. And it was scythed right out of the nest, just as it was growing its first stalk, its first leaves. It was scythed and pierced by an alien tree because humans thought it to be superior, a civilized tree, see, the good kind that bears real sweet fruit, profitable, a normal tree, basic. They mutilated the rootstock. They cut the tree. They wanted to murder it from within. And so the tree hurled itself at me that day. It hurled itself at my entire race of lime-tree torturers. Trees know revenge better than any of us. They chew on it. One day, they'll stop blooming and they'll watch us croak. Look, look here, my arms, my back. I kept these scars. I will keep them for my entire life. And it's my sister, Édith. My scar. It'll never go away, you see? It won't go away. Truth be told, that's where I was really born, on the enraged thorns of a grafted lime tree."

And as if to avenge the wound that is our childhood, Kim strangles in his hands the carcasses of the wild limes. He picks each seed and pinches it between his thumb and index finger. His long phalanges peel back the tegument, extract the cotyledon and purge it until there is nothing left.

Ayo leans her silence over Kim's exhausted body. She observes him. She meets him. She drinks him. She places her Breath on Kim's forehead and holds his gaze. He doesn't really see her, but she, from the edge of the world, flowing on the shore of mist-filled ethers, melts in the child's saturnine eyes, and she says: "This mouth that speaks to trounce the whole universe is mine. These cheeks that stretch in an infinite wait for a deferred kiss are mine. This nose that opens itself to the palimpsestic humus of humanity is mine. This child is mine." And the whole world fades away to let the ancestor's soul pour what's left of massacred memories on this weary brow. She wants to tell him: "Hero, don't you dare waver." She wants to shake him, to extract from this body the poison of hatred and to restore it to its grandeur. So Ayo seizes the arms of the wicker rocking chair and spills a dissonant scream on her descendant to wake him up. But Kim doesn't hear her.

It's four in the morning, night dwellers are swarming in the Régale neighborhood. At the bromeliad's chalice, each frog sings to her neighbor the tale of her night. From the leafy shelters where they hang, crickets lend a delicate ear to the hushed gospel of their predators. And the nocturnal flowers, in slow vibrations, transmit the message to the slumbering trees. They awaken and rustle with surprise, swelling the entire tropical selva with a symphony of gossip. With this intense *makrelaj*, the night dwellers know more about Kim than the living and the dead do. These dwellers call out to me, me, who has become one with the walls' memory, sitting on the world's shore, where the present no longer exists, where all epistemes meet, where hearts no longer beat but are still aglow. I abandon my ear to the crackling of this frightful night, and carried by the frogs' insistent threnody, my soul leaves the *kaz* and hurtles down the *morne*.

To Hush the Frogs Now

IT'S FOUR IN THE MORNING. Far from here, near *lanvil*-downtown, close, very close to the ocher checkerboard that is the island's capital, a pack of dogs catches the scent of blood, and with their paws up on a wall, they yip terrible yaps fit to scare the cockroaches away. Their cohorts from the Dillon neighborhood nearby attempt to decipher amid the morning's serenade if the canine alarm tolls for the buffet or the tocsin. For their part, the frogs already know the whole tale. Wedged in the walls' cracks, they saw the assassin kill in silence, with a butcher's knife, in the middle of the afternoon. They read in his eyes the depth of a long-planned gesture, for it wasn't a sudden rage, no, it wasn't a crime borne out of the instant: it was an ambush, a mission, a terrible sentence dealt by a cold, determined being. They saw him, that young man, turn his gaze away from the growing puddle of blood and leave with neither regret nor shame. And since then, the frogs have been holding a wake for the lifeless flesh, waiting for the necrophagous insects on which they will feast come nighttime. It's four in the morning and, with their bellies taut by the putrid dessert, the frogs whistle a strange tune that irritates the dogs. Professional *makrel*-gossips, they spill the story to the wind, and very slowly, the story climbs the slope that leads to the city against the current. The hissing follows the asphalt of the four-lane highway first, skirting the edges of the sugarcane field, the lands polluted by chlordecone and what is left of the mangroves. Having reached the south, the chant scales the green hills, the *mornes*, and swells in a rivulet of the Régale neighborhood. And in the valley where Kim holed himself up, this valley stretched by the moon's iron, the frogs narrate the previous day's mush to their neighbors. So on the veranda of the *kaz*, so close to the assassin, the Régale frogs sing their city sisters' macabre dinner and await their turn. Patiently.

Ayo, too, listens to the frogs. She recognizes Kim in their noisy tales, and now she knows what he's done. She knows that Kim killed my son Cédric, whose cadaver lies on the cold tile of my kitchen at the edge of *lanvil*. Beneath the diaphanous skin of Ayo's belly writhes the void left by the baby she tried to pluck from existence two hundred years ago. Her belly writhes over this being who should not have lived but did, born under the eye of four colonists who smoked while delighting in the animal spectacle of a *Négresse* foaling in a stable.

When she was still alive, Ayo had helped end pregnancies for dozens of *Négresses* from the plantations of southern Martinique. Her art was renowned from François to Rivière Pilote, and from the Atlantic Ocean to the Caribbean coast. She enlisted smugglers sworn to silence to transport her remedies along the sugar roads. In the folds of their rags, they hid justicia secunda leaves rolled in collard dove feces, which they would have to swallow should they get caught. From hand to hand, the merchandise reached the one whose name was spoken, and then the women of the Black Shack Alley took turns watching over the parturient until the black gold of her belly flowed as a scarlet brine right out of men's hell. When the pregnancy was too far along, Ayo herself marooned after nightfall to the bedside of the resistant, to add sungrass to the remedy and paint a door to the other world on the wall. And the fetuses crossed over. Ayo had never failed. But none of her plants and even less her blood vévés had succeeded in dissuading that child. Hers.

Until then, the masters had never minded their talented healer's poisoning rituals. With her infallible discretion, she would decimate their rivals' cattle, and as far as they knew, she wouldn't have dared suppress the unborn children of her own plantation. So with a silent complicity tinged with a dash of adventurism, the masters never denounced Ayo. But faced with the relentlessness with which she tried to kill her already far-along fetus, they panicked. No, they would not let this poison spread on their plantation and risk the same ruin as their neighbors, for if a woman could kill her own child, there was no telling how far she could go. Perhaps she'd soon dare attack her mistress or make her forever barren before stealing the life of every man in the household in one single night? The doubt was enough to keep them awake at night. As her term was coming to an end, the masters imprisoned Ayo, shackled her, and waited to claim their due, their fleshy commodity, alive, to sell it to the highest bidder. Separated from her plants and spells, Ayo still tried. Even in that last interminable hour, she attempted to tighten all the muscles of her sex around the body of the child, hoping to smother him. She recited all the incantations that would supposedly make him be born strangled. She funneled the most noxious gases she inhaled to her womb to suffocate him. At last, she laughed a delirious laughter, remembering, cynical, the voice of the witch who had initiated her inside the hold of the slave ship between Dahomey and Martinique. At the departure with no return, Ayo was but an apprentice, barely out of childhood. The witch protected her from the brigands' greedy gaze by draping her in a spell, and during the entire passage, she taught Ayo everything she knew, like a litany of words erected against death. And to prolong her protection and reward her disciple's consecration, the witch promised Ayo her progeny would never know slavery. She howled her spell in her native tongue just before setting herself ablaze on the ship's deck.

Yet fifteen years later, Ayo was well and truly pregnant with a being who would not be expelled from her womb. And even killing him at birth, they would not let her. Born cursed, desecrated, the child was jerked from his matrix by libidinous hands and transplanted to a foreign breast. Unnamed. Lost.

Accused of using poisons, Ayo was not delivered to the overly merciful hands of colonial justice. With their neighbors as witnesses, the masters tied her with leather straps to the thorny trunk of a kapok tree until her own life spilled out along with her blood in the clay soil. Although she was freed from this hell, Ayo didn't cross over to the other world. She had prepared her escape to a shore from which she could continue her mission, because the war wasn't over, because she needed to transmit to a child the knowledge that could dry out the serpents' blood once and for all. She remained in the in-between-worlds, and from there, she searched for her son. For a long time. She found his body in the forest one day. He was already ripe and dead.

And here he is, the child, here he is, found again two hundred years later in another life. Why? To watch him kill his own blood? To watch him wait for death while sobering up? To watch him slash with a knife the lineage she had not managed to abort? And for whom, now? For what? How did death get the season so wrong? Ayo howls, and her howl awakens the other ghosts hanging from the branches of the kapok tree.

Kim hears a blood-curdling scream. Startled, he awakens. "Who is there?" He leaps, runs, nearly falls. In his stomach, a ball of lead snuffs his thoughts out. He runs and finds himself away from the hostage, too far away, stuck in a dark room under a pile of clothes or under a sink, maybe. He holds the knife with both hands, stupidly cutting himself and mixing his blood with his victims'. His heart beats fast. He listens carefully to the world, balls his fist up so tight it bleeds, and even his teeth chatter.

Kim is afraid.

He whistles uncontrollably between his clenched jaws. There, in the ray of light that crosses the main room and caresses the hallway, he can see the doors of the living room and he waits for a brigade a contingent a regiment to take him away to gas him smoke him shoot him kill him. He could die. He doesn't want to die. He learns right then and there that he doesn't want to die.

But nothing. Nothing but darkness in this hallway.

Kim puts himself back together, thinks about his hostage, extricates himself from under the ton of dirty clothes, and quickly returns to the living room to put his knife on Laurent's neck. There, tensed like a mongoose with all senses on high alert, he probes the depths of the night. He hears the scream once more but soothes his heart adrift with a deep sigh. "It is not time yet. It's just an alarm, you fool! It's just a frog singing! *Fout man boulé.* I am too drunk."

The serene morning wind blows on Kim and makes him shudder. Appeased, he lets go of Laurent's head, which rolls back. Kim slap-slaps his own two cheeks, jumps up and down, clears his throat. Ayo tries to seize hold of her son at this moment. The living are more porous to the world of the deceased when they're afraid of dying. She breathes on the open curtains and runs a cold air down Kim's back, which makes him take a step forward. He comes to the window. He puts both elbows on the sill. The window opens onto the heights of Régale. The window opens onto the land of our childhood, and Ayo takes him back to where it all began.

To Return Under the Mango Tree

THE MOON AND THE SUN QUARREL for the right to rise. On one end of the valley, the moon is round and her gray dress turns red. Across from her, the sun quietly awakens the contours of the *morne*. At the bottom of the valley, the haze swells and gives Régale the allure of a wild island. From the window, Kim caresses the *morne*'s curve with his knife. He knows this flank by heart. As a child, he climbed it a hundred times. Through eyes still misty, he pictures each tall tree, each talus, each perched shack. "Well, look what we have here! The *béké*'s old house is still occupied," he marvels, rediscovering the white walls of an old colonial house with an impeccable profile, lit with paper lanterns. It was Kim's secret refuge. He would go up there with our cousins on Sundays. Right out of mass, their ears still ringing from the patriarchal sect's sermons, the children would feverishly swap pressed dresses and starched shirts for old *dédou*-rags. Before anyone could tell them otherwise, they would vanish from the street, vanish from the neighborhood, doing wheelies on bikes that were either too tall or too small but always fast enough.

Kim's knife retraces in the air this path he knows by heart, the one that crisscrosses the *morne*. He remembers the hours spent there with his cousins, just a few steps away from this domineering house, under the *béké*'s mango tree, without permission without invitation, his heart beating with a diffuse fear. Kim and his cousins were *malfinis*, bona fide Caribbean hawks, audacious, proud, highest among the highest, laying claim to their domain, the Lamentin Valley stretching before their eyes. Over there, the sugarcane fields, endless and flattened, to the West one sea and to the East the other, competing for the hardest blue, and way beyond, the Pitons, which, from this vantage point, looked like the open thighs of a woman. Kim and his cousins would contemplate them for a moment without speaking or while listening to Eugène Mona's voice on their Walkman as he hymned the names of the *bwa brilé*, Otis Redding, Louis Armstrong, all Black folks given White names on this land. And when the owner's dogs would yap them back to reality, silly reality, the mischievous band of rascals would spill down the hill laughing and run back to Maman's home.

And like that, exiting alcohol through the door of memory, Kim is swooshed back to the dark angular silhouette of our childhood home. His fist tightens around a recollection. Kim pushes it away and distracts himself by dreaming of the garden he loved so much.

Upon returning from his virile escapades with our cousins, Kim would always make himself presentable for his mother. Near a massive bay rum tree that gave the wash a singular fragrance, Maman had suspended a shower tiled with ceramic fragments. On this improbable mosaic, which, in fact, traced incantations, water would meet the body, dress itself with its dust before running along in the garden, all the way to the roots of the lime tree. The water was warm as it rushed out of pipes just beneath the earth's surface. But idleness being frowned upon in this land, the liquid would quickly turn frigid on the skin, grab hold of the child, always by surprise, and twist him in a shudder. It was always over quick. Nothing was ever wasted. Maman never installed a water heater: it was part of a conspiracy against laziness, which always lay in wait for her children.

Kim would pat his skin with a large towel and run to his bedroom to escape mosquitoes. And then Kim would slip into an old pair of pajamas. And Maman would comb the hair of her wild youngest daughter. Early, very early, night would stretch her arms around the *kaz*. It was the hour between two meals when things were told. If there was nothing to say, Maman and Kim would sit in front of the TV. Maman would let some tomfoolery drone away on Channel One, some program from France-France, the only kinds of programs available, really, or some reality TV.

Kim smiles. Kim forgets. He gives himself over to Maman, who sings an old tale that only the women of her blood know. Kim tells it to Laurent. "For it is in the roots of your black hair that all the power rests. For it is the whirlwind of your dark curls that ciphers our secret. For it is in the storm of your rising locks that the seal of our silence will break."

Ayo holds her child in her arms. But he doesn't know it. She wrote this song. Ayo thinks it sounds better in her tongue. It's her great-granddaughter Léonide who translated it into French. She would sing it just like that while doing Kim's grandmother's hair. And all the secrets shared from mouth to mouth, from African ports across the Atlantic would rush between the teeth of her comb.

1952. The sun, tall, shines on the sculpted handle. Léonide can't stand the sight of her hands. She pulls on the comb a little too hard, the child screams. She composes herself. She wouldn't want to hurt her. The child is Sidonie, our grandmother. I recognize on her cheek the mango-shaped rune that furrowed her dimple. Léonide wishes she could love Sidonie as she deserves to be loved. She wishes she could stop seeing in her daughter's face the face of the man who tore her apart for five francs on Liberation Day. She survived it. She must now survive the memory of it. To gird her loins, she breathes and recites these words that will spare her daughter from the hell that keeps rising back from the depths of time: "For it is in the roots of your black hair that all the power rests. For it is the whirlwind of your dark curls that ciphers our secret. For it is in the storm of your rising locks that the seal of our silence will break."

In the *kaz*, Ayo exhales a chilly wind as she listens to the lost child who doesn't know, who no longer knows who he is, as he sings her own oath. She seals it, and now, she whispers. She says: Child, you are lost, but you will not die tonight.

The spell twists Kim's organs, and his body purges itself. Kneeling in his own bile, he spins, he flails around inside himself, he falls apart, beat-beat-beating his fist still balled up tight around his weapon. On the verge of blacking out, he tells himself that it would perhaps be easier to slip away. He tells himself that perhaps the alcohol is lying, that perhaps he is already dead. Only the forest's music confirms that he is still alive. Only the cold gaze of his hostage leads him to believe that he is not alone in confronting his crime. So he picks himself back up, seizes hold of this gaze and pounces on it like someone grabbing onto a life preserver:

"Laurent! Laurent! Listen. Listen to the last songs of the night. It's poetry. All these creatures and their endless whistles that pierce your head even when you dream. It's the sentinels' song. The frogs hold the sun hostage. That's it! And they make such a ruckus that the sun won't dare escape from the ocean. Listen! This music is immaculate. It is grace incarnate offered to the land of the humans. Amen. Silence . . . Silence is trash. That's right. Silence is a fabrication. Already in the belly of your mother, there's a ruckus. Well, that's nature. Nature is sound! And I drank so much that I can hear it in stereo! Listen to the frogs' song. Listen to them, Laurent. Do you feel it? Do you feel it coursing through your veins? Are your arteries pulsating? Are they boiling? Yes? You feel it? There! That's Martinique. That's Martinique. It's . . . a cacophony of sweet songs."

Kim is on the veranda, violently swaying. He plucks a twig in between his slender fingers and brandishes it toward the sky. Legs akimbo, he beats the rhythm into the teak floor with his foot and begins a symphony, conducting the whole world. Frogs on brass, crickets on violins, and *cabrit-bwas* on drums! He rummages through his childhood for the terrible torments that put his knife in this sinister trance. He rummages through old nursery rhymes to find the already blurry reason why it all started. He finds nothing: Only his body knows, and his body is gone. But he sings. He sings. "*Mets des robes qui soient jolies, mé pa povotjé sé nonm-lan! Sé zot menm ki ka chèché'y, é aprè zot ka pléré! Ma manman m'a dit! A pa mwen ki di ki di!** Sing, Laurent! It's a gift from the sky, this water that unravels its ribbons on the valley, look! Sing, I want to hear your voice! Why don't you sing, Laurent? Laurent!

* "Put on pretty dresses, but don't tease boys! You're the ones looking for trouble, and then you cry! My mama told me! I didn't say it, say it!" A Eugène Mona song.

To Kill Dread

DREAD RUSHES ACROSS the living room. Kim returns in a flash.

"Ooooay! *An milpat!* I crushed it, didn't I? Look at how pitiful he looks, right there, under my foot. Piece of shit! The fuck are you doing with those slippers on, Laurent? This is the countryside, you crusty old bourgeois! You need real soles when you live here! Something real tough! You never know when you'll have to crush a cockroach! It's you or him, don't you know? I hate these critters. They're everywhere. I know because I grew up not far from here, in Régale. Régale, you know it, don't you? Nah, nah, you think you know, but you don't . . . You'll never know Régale, the real one. It's the land of brave folks. You, you're just a coward. I'm sure you never dared set foot there. That's why you don't know me. If you'd dared come to Régale, you'd know who I am. You'd know that my feet are as hard as the stones I raked as a child. And yours? Baby skin? Baby feet are good for nothing. It's just insect candy, and when you're underground, that's what they'll start chewing on first. I know this land. This land is my skin, my root. I'm not afraid of it. Look at me! I'm not stretched toward the sky to masticate its clouds. I am not a cathedral steeple, I am a colossus planted in the earth. I am the anchor of my own ship. I don't roll. I don't pitch. No. I am fastened to the land, I have power, power! There's no pushing power around. It doesn't let itself be crushed by centuries of shackles, it doesn't let itself be chewed on by maggots, it fights back. I'm taking up arms, yes! This knife is the arm of all my foremothers, heroic, intense, free! And today, I am the one, I am the power. I am the one, I am putting an end to the story, to history. Me, I know where I'm from. I'm from there, from the land, from Régale, from Kongo, from clay, sand, reg. Me! But you, you're from nowhere because your feet are caked in talcum, they no longer brave the ground, they brave nothing at all! They're growing soft in their cotton slippers!"

A cephalgia overwhelms Kim and his breath. He feels for the wall behind him and brings one hand to his thorax. Panic. Beads of sweat dawn on his broad forehead where veins trace grooves for the rivers of resentment that burden his soul. Kim stumbles, picks his heart up with his belly in knots, and clings to his bloody knife as if it were an anchor. His gaze is now fixed on Laurent.

Ayo changes the cold sweat that drips on her descendant's aged face into beads of salt. How she wishes he would taste this salt to feel the water rush into his fathers' lungs in the ocean of the in-between-worlds. How she wishes Kim would hear, in this salty cry, the hope for a better life. How she wishes she could tell him, Go, little one, go build the life for which your mothers died, for which your mothers were raped, for which your mothers were mutilated. Don't avenge them, no, so that their sacrifice may make at least one happy soul on this earth. Go, so that you may one day see a joyous fearless little girl grow between your hands. And you, you'll know perhaps better than anyone how to stop death, because your blood knows it so well, because your eyes have faced it and defied it before you were even born, before you even existed. How Ayo wishes she could tell him, Look, no malediction is born without remedy. How she wishes she could tell him, Word, no spell can be lifted by taking a life. How she wishes she could tell him, at last, You are too ignorant of the mysteries of the world. Death is too happy a remedy for the torments of humans. There are other ones, there are better ones, there are stronger ones. How is it possible that you still don't know? Is it because you are a boy wherefore they forgot to tell you the secrets of your own lineage?

But Kim still can't hear her. Kim has never heard her. Perhaps it's true, they should have initiated Kim, they should have shown him how to reach the shores of the dead mothers. Then maybe he could have talked to Ayo, and maybe, yes, he would not have taken a life to try to save his own.

"Eugène Mona died like that," Kim recalls while taking a sip of *madou*. "Eugène Mona. The singer. He was swept away by a bad rage. If they ever erect his statue, as they damn well should, they'll have to make it out of pure rage, to grasp his life. Mona. I drink to your health up there! Perhaps soon, we'll toast together."

Ayo has seen these eyes before, wildly worried in their black shells, shaking, bloodshot. These are the eyes of the suicides. So, terrified, Ayo slips back into the shadow and lets Kim dance in the *kaz*. It's five in the morning, and Ayo rushes to find me before I awake, before I turn on the radio, before I hear the news. She wants to divert my anger and prevent me at least from killing my own brother.

To Satisfy the *Makrels*

IN FORT-DE-FRANCE, the world wakes up early. Martinique is lived, alive, as early as the blue hour when the day has yet to be born but already wails in the haze that births it. Soon, the flow of cars coming from the south will flood the air with a purring ruckus. Soon, their dust will cover the *lanvil*-downtown neighborhoods with a malevolent dome. Soon, noise will be the empire of humans, and in this howl, the sun will flood the capital. But at the blue hour, in the suburbs, birds still reign on the branches of the mango trees. They weave a sweet melody in the fresh air, a caress bestowed upon the space that echoes all the way to the other worlds. In Fort-de-France, this calm song accompanies the steps of the workers, the men and women who toil in the cool morning air. They clean, tidy, build, protect, and sanitize the world that the people from the south must fructify. The world doesn't go round without those making the rounds in the morning. The men know it, the women know it, and there they are in the calm. Sometimes, the workers whistle and worry the birds with their facetious human whistling. More often, however, they walk in silence, already absorbed in their day. Every day, the same ballet of boots, worn-out sneakers, and lost canes. And in the humble silence of humans, the smell of coffee.

<<< >>>

The neighborhood knows by heart the morning rituals. But that morning, in Dillon, the dogs yap a little too early. Their untimely din disrupts my neighbor Georgette's quotidian minute of morning contemplation. She peels her eyes away from the reassuring gurgle of her coffee percolator and turns her thick frame toward the still-shut kitchen window. A large black butterfly is beached on the sill, where it awaits its own death. Bad omen. Georgette gets up from her chair, frowns, swallows a curse word, and opens her shutters.

The sun is already spreading over the borough and stretching the shadow of my house across the street. The dogs have congregated there into a pack, their muzzles trained toward the kitchen window. Someone ought to open that window and shoo them away already. As Georgette thinks this, the bread delivery car honks as it rounds the corner. It stops right in front of my door. The driver waits. He delivers Creole bread to my house every morning. Georgette is next. She puts on her sandals, adjusts her sarong around her heavy bosom, and tightens her *maré tèt*-headscarf around her half-twisted buns. And then she comes out, to get her bread and finally assess with her own two eyes the sonorous soundscape that sends the little street into spasms. The delivery man honks a raspy honk and, with the car in neutral, glides toward Georgette, who came further out than usual to greet him.

"What's going on next door?" she asks without preliminaries.

"Bonjour Georgette."

"*Bel bonjou, bel bonjou!*"

"There's no one. But Frédéric's car is there. Maybe everyone is asleep?"

"And the dogs?"

From the corner of her eye, the *makrel*-gossipmonger catches a glimpse of her morning gossip sisters waiting for the scene to unfold, each one hidden behind her blinds. Secretly taking them as her witnesses, she stares at the delivery man with one of those looks that command without a word. "I'll go see," he replies, heading toward the pack. In the blink of an eye, the dogs scatter and line up on the opposite curb, their tails as straight as exclamation marks. In this neighborhood, low houses dwell in the shadow of apartment buildings. The folks who live here are not very rich, but they have small gardens and garages. Sure, it gets hot in the afternoon under the tin roofs, but at least you don't have to share your steps and your troubles with four other neighboring families like in the big apartment complexes. And this morning, it's in one of those low houses that the whole world is about to poke its nose.

The bread man is on tiptoes against the yellowish wall of my house, where the window stayed shut. He grabs the iron grate and pulls himself up to see inside. And he doesn't call out. He stares at a gray body, throat slit, floating in a dark blood slick. A rat sniffs around the arm of the cadaver, a man between two ages. Beyond, another body stares at him with a blank gaze, mouth agape, thirsty for air. The bread man recognizes my son, Cédric. He will never sleep again. He's aged as he climbs down the wall, and his eyes are empty when he tells the *makrel*:

"The devil has come. We are without a country now."

To Be on Television

BACK IN THE *KAZ*, Laurent was not singing, so Kim turned on the TV. Trace FM, dancehall and bare-assed girls. He turns up the volume and draws from the testosterone-filled tunes the energy to turn the place upside down. With the booming bass, this pandemonium could awaken the dead mothers of the kapok tree. Kim dances on the rug, playing with his knife. He rediscovers in his legs an ancient strength that climbs up to his hips and dares him to survive, in spite of it all. A heap of mattresses wood and broken glass blockades the sliding door. Kim shouldn't even see the sunrise.

"There! They can come now. I am waiting for them." Laurent gawps at the TV screen. That's so him: watching the game while wifey keeps busy in the kitchen. Kim pulls his rocking chair next to the sofa, real close to Laurent. Even at this early hour, one can become dumber watching just about anything: telenovelas, porn, crime shows, news on a loop . . . there is something for everyone. Kim grabs the remote, turns up the volume and channel surfs.

"Me too, I'll be on TV. The only way to get them to notice you is to do something very bad. You think I did something very bad yesterday, Laurent? Nah! I did something serious, but it wasn't bad. No. I'll be on TV. And I'll explain why they had to die. But not while I'm drunk. It'll have to wait until I sober up. It will be a nice change from those dumb reality shows. I watched them all, all the original ones, you remember? *Big Brother*, *Star Academy*. Ah, the good ol' days of the beginning of the end of the world. I saw Loana fuck in the swimming pool in a pre-recorded live. Well, actually, I didn't really see anything because, at that exact moment, Maman ferociously pushed my head down so that she could comb the little hairs at the nape of my neck that hadn't even been bothering anybody. My two butt cheeks sank painfully into the old cushion that was only dragged out for our hair care rituals. It elevated us just enough for our skulls to be at elbow height for Maman. The TV spewed its shit, and we listened to the TV and Maman. She was the one who translated White people TV for us, who educated us on White people TV."

Kim isn't really listening to Laurent's oversized screen. He is between Maman's knees, his legs folded up against his chest in the delicious cocoon of childhood. Maman says:

"People really don't know how to behave correctly. *Tjip!* You can see that girl's whole entire panties! Just try to come in front of me dressed like that one day, you'd best believe you'd have to find somewhere else to sleep."

"Maman . . . I can't hear what they're saying . . ."

"Stop moving, Kim! You don't need to hear that. They're talking nonsense."

Maman held a grudge against the French, or at least that was how Kim remembered her dealings with White people. She only watched *Big Brother* to get mad.

"Oh! Look: *ER*." Kim pauses on a channel. "You know, Laurent, Maman was madly in love with Dr. Kovak, a Kosovan or something like that; he was from a place that had never done anything to us, and that was enough to make him attractive. Well, that's my interpretation, maybe she just found him handsome. I don't know,

I didn't see much of the series. When Maman did my hair, instead of letting my eyes wander, I closed them. Anyway, I didn't need to see the TV. I listened to the screen in Maman's mouth. I loved it when she combed my hair. I loved it. She probably knew it, and I think she loved it, too. It was a moment with just her and just me. Between her and me."

Maybe it's for her. Maybe it's for her that Kim killed. For Maman. Because as a child, Kim's silence made him guilty. For Maman, because she would have done the same thing had she known. For Maman, because he hopes that she, at least, will understand him. For the words we never said to each other but that could capsize the whole world. He killed for her. Or at least, maybe that's what he thinks.

I am not in my body when the judge addresses me. I am not there. The words she exchanges with my lawyer bounce against my eardrums before flying off into the folds of my memory. I take my leave to survive in a burrow of my being where this ordeal never happened, where Cédric is still this warm little being against my belly who laughs at simple jokes and hands me his scribbles. I am not mad, I do not offer my rage to Kim. I look him in the eyes when he speaks to me, and I leave. Where I go, above my body, I feel nothing but void and silence. I am not in pain: I cannot feel pain for a tragedy I will not allow to exist. But tomorrow, I will no longer be able to hush that memory. Nor the others, for that matter. Up on the stand, I will have to say what I feel. Kim did that, he forces me to live that, he forces me to make real the memories I had exiled.

Kim says he wants to do me justice at the trial. He is not crazy. He believes, as one believes in God, that the blood of his victims was a just sacrifice. He wants this trial to give back to our mothers their bodies their skin their hands their slashed wrists their choked throats their torn vulvae their gutted entrails their hearts that no longer beat. By detailing the reasons for his crimes, he wants to put on trial all the criminals who shackled his genes. And he believes he will be forgiven in the end because he killed in cold blood to avenge the blood of his foremothers.

It won't be a trial. Kim wants it to be the last judgment of a story that lasted too long. He thinks that this punishment will spark the last struggle for justice. He sees no other way out but war. War: that immense word that begets real revolutions in the world. Kim believes, deep in the deafening drumming of his heart, that war is the only door behind which a free country awaits, one worth dying for.

That's what Kim pretends anyway on visiting days. But here, in the *kaz,* sitting close to Laurent, I see him doubt. He doubts that the world is ready for such truths. He doubts that he will even be allowed to talk at his trial. "They don't know. They don't know their story, their history. They don't know how to listen to the Breaths. They never pay tribute to their ancestors. They drank the words of the Whites, accepted the law of forgetting. They won't hear anything because they love to shield their ears from the shitstorm of history. They don't know that heroes were born from this storm! Those people, those people made small, ignorant, they won't understand a thing. But they'll listen to you, Laurent. You'll tell them. Your body will tell them! You'll see, you, the whole you, you'll show them that their universe is on the brink of collapse! I have big plans for the two of us. You'll be part of history, you too, by the time I'm done, Laurent, you'll see. And you'll be able to say, on the day you die, that you will have finally been good for something."

To Enter the Sanctuary

FAR AWAY, ON THE ISLAND'S ATLANTIC COAST, Ayo appears at my doorstep. Me, Édith, her descendant. Édith, her heir. Édith, the survivor. Carried by the Breaths to the remembrance of that night, I am there, too, and hidden in the walls of my own home, my errant spirit becomes the indiscreet spectator of my own memory.

I live in Dillon during the week, but all my weekends are devoted to this home lulled by the rustle of the ocean. Macabou is where I am nestling our new sanctuary. I am building it in secret. I invite to my ceremonies the souls of the ancestors who died in the ocean and pray to them to help me move the door to the in-between-worlds, for it is beyond my power. With their Breaths as nourishment, I mix my blood with pigments in sacred calabashes to paint this gate on a living room wall. I dedicate my Saturdays to this task, and to finance it, I hold séances on Sundays, concealed behind a wax print drape that separates me from my clients. Nobody knows I am a *kimbwaseuse*, a conjure woman, not even Kim. It's too dangerous, for me a little, but, above all, for my son. I don't want him to be teased at school.

<<< >>>

Everyone in the little town knows my house. I said I lived there with an African marabout, that I helped him concoct essential oils. It's a bit of a strange wooden house with a view of the ocean, drowned in a forest of bizarre plants.

Ayo frowns as she approaches the walls. She needs to talk to me, but I am asleep on this clear night, at peace, with no obligation to anyone. The scent of *belles de nuit*-jalapas spills into my room. I lie exhausted by a Saturday that my body has not yet cast into the depths of the mattress. I needed to float off-world in a wordless and colorless coma. So the night before, I had turned off my phone, drunk a passiflora decoction, unburdened myself from the entirety of the mental load this ungrateful tribe makes me carry, and that morning, hermetic to the Breaths' screams, I am completely given over to one of those sleeps most people only dream of.

But Ayo must find a way to pry me from this respite before Kim, in his suicidal flight, destroys everything his ancestors built. But she cannot enter my home without a proper invitation: I protected the doors of my sanctuary from the other flying spirits. Ayo could try to pass through the door I am drawing in blood in my living room, but it is not complete. So she is stuck at my stoop for as long as I sleep. And time is precious.

On the landing of the dark home, the ground is sandy and cool. Ayo roots down with the entire weight of her soul and begins to dance. She conjures up blood to save her child. She conjures up the blood lost in that sea that laps the shore a few paces away from here. Knees bent, back straight, hips open, she stomps her foot to awaken the fallen spirits. Her worn-out heel hits the sandy ground of my garden in cadence with the heart and the loins of the earth. The bodies of the Kalinagos buried there under her feet awaken. Their blood is there, spilled in the mud of the people who lived there long ago. The world's rootstock that had been implanted there twists and turns to erupt into the powerful leg of the witch.

The people of the land below the land know Ayo. The witch has always healed bodies and soothed souls. No one dares deny her passage. But the frog who has become my devoted sentinel here in Macabou sees in Ayo nothing but a potential criminal. So she stands tall on my stoop in front of this presumptuous ghost whom she doesn't know and swells, swells, and asks: "Who are you to dare approach the door between the two worlds?" Without batting an eyelid, Ayo replies to the immense frog:

"I am Ayo, witch of the Dahomey, initiated in the knowledge of the between life and death by my mothers and their mothers. I was captured by brigands in 1811 of the Christian era on the coasts of my land. On the boat, there were eight hundred of us. Two hundred sank in the ocean right there behind you. Two hundred, including the evacuated bodies of the innocents I saved from slavery. They returned to the land of their ancestors, carried by the Breaths. But I sailed across. When we docked, I had to leave the magic cocoon another witch had woven to cloak me from the monsters' gaze, and for the first time, a White man laid eyes on me and made me into a Black woman, marking my skin with a blazing lash. 'Move,' he said. And on this here land you call Martinique, I talked to the soil, I awoke Hairun's volcano with the heel of my foot.* You know me, old frog: the volcano howled when I walked here for the first time. I was just a child. I had already saved thirty of my kin. The sea is my witness. I have always been a priestess here, since the first day, since the first step. I am the one who drew the first door to the in-between-worlds. So you know me before even knowing me. I must pass through and be on my way. Open for me. Édith is my daughter. It is for her that I have come."

The sentinel frog seeks counsel from her peers in the world of the dead. They tell her of Ayo in the Christian year 1812, on the

* Hairun is the Kalinago name of Saint Vincent, a volcanic island south of Martinique.

Place de l'Enregistrement, the square where they sold African flesh into labor. Ayo, overwhelmed by the tidal waves of moaning and human suffering, lifted her chin to the sky and ordered the wind and the volcanoes to begin the end of times. So Hairun's volcano spewed its entrails into the sky. So the sky rained black tears on the golden fields. Hoarsely, the masters inhaled the murderous dust. It grew tumors in the hearts of children, elderly men, and the living zombies who walked in the dark. You couldn't see anything. But the volcanic ash couldn't stop the music of the whip at the foot of the giant floating coffins. Ayo cursed the sun. And Ayo cursed this muddy shore of viscous dust. And Ayo cursed the White man who had made her a Black woman. He died shortly after. Pulmonary embolism.

As she awaits the frog's decision, Ayo dances in the moonlight to prepare her spell. She bends her knees on the embers and casts into the earth the power of her living kin. There, in the *fondok* of her belly, deep deep, dwell all the ones she was and all the ones she conceived. In the fold of her vagina in trance, life, renewed, sways its hips, an excess of pleasure that hadn't had a chance to name itself before expiring. "Breath!" Ayo calls upon the woman who turned her to dust in the hold of the slave ship to veil her from the libidinous gaze of the White man who fed them. That old Kongo priestess knew that Ayo would not die. That priestess knew that Ayo could not die. She concealed her from the world of the Whites so that she could rise like an army upon arrival. So in the shadow of the female quarters of the slave ship's hold, the Kongo witch shared with Ayo the secrets that decide the lives of some and the deaths of others. The priestess sanctified Ayo and committed her entire lineage to the service of the Breaths who transport deported souls back to their land.

In the hold, there was no room on the floor to draw the vévés that linked the priestess to the spirits of death. So she would mix her blood with the flour fed to the sequestered bodies, and she would draw waves and shores on the ship's walls, in a trance carried by murmured songs. This vévé was the door to the in-between-worlds. She would lay every child born on this seal, and he would disappear. That's how, without poison, she sent the souls of the martyrs back to African lands.

Ayo stomps. The ground in the distance awakens a volcano. "Breath!" she screams to the wind. Her chest open to the crying ocean, Ayo howls in her heart the memory of the one who taught her everything and who died ablaze on the deck of a drunken boat.

"Breath!" Ayo's arms send to the East and to the West the call of her brothers and sisters resting at the bottom of the ocean. The sacred invocation covers the entire earth when, in a roar, she stretches her neck toward the sky and stomps and stomps the ground again enough to awaken all the volcanoes!

Hairun's volcano tells the frog to let the priestess through. The frog isn't sure, but she lets her through anyway.

To Snuff Out the Morning Light

"DON'T YOU DARE judge my mother, Laurent!"

In the *kaz*, Kim works himself up. He asks the questions and spits the answers. "All this shit on TV, it was good for her. You'd want to empty your head, too, if you worked at a bank. She wasn't at the counter chitchatting either, no. Maman, she crunched numbers all day. But she never complained, Maman. She earned enough for the three of us, and we always had what we needed. As you see me, *ou konprann mwen sé an vakabon?* Because I killed, you think I grew up in the streets? No. Not me. I never wanted for anything. Maman gave us everything. Everything. She birthed every day, every sun, and every moon, too. Maman never took a day off from her children, no, she was a lifer. In the house, we'd hear her footsteps nonstop. They gave the beat to the day's rhythm. We were always in slow motion next to her. Maman cooks. Maman washes. Maman tidies up. Maman phones her girlfriends as she cooks washes tidies up. Maman gardens. Maman mends. Maman balances her checkbook and the paper screeches beneath her angry old pen. She sure balanced that checkbook. We never wanted for anything, I tell you! She was never thick, Maman, she exercised all day! And when she'd go out at night with her girlfriends, with her starry lips and her butterfly eyes, her cascading extensions and that dress that made everyone dizzy, whoay! Maman could dance all night, and the next day, her feet would clack around the kitchen, all the same. Actually, I think she must have rested at work, otherwise, I can't see when . . . Right, that's why those government workers are slow like that, it's because the women don't sleep at home. They have to sleep somewhere. She didn't smile much. But she was proud. Her stern face was a portrait of power. When you crossed the threshold of her house, she was the queen of her domain. The home in Régale was the lady's palace. She could tell the rain to fall. And it would."

And every morning, up there in Régale, our life started with the *pipiri*-kingbird's song. Kim never told anyone, but his eyes were always already open when dawn crept in. It was at this very time, exactly. When the hens awaken, when the world slowly starts to keel over into the light, that's when everything started, when everything started again, again and again. Kim never missed that moment either, no. Never. And since then, the song has never left him, it has branded his skin forever.

Kim hears the bird flutter its wings in the garden's darkness, then he opens his eyelids. And he remains there, on the lookout, waiting, his arms long against his body. He says:

"My heart beats fast."

It beats the rhythm of a warrior's march, a dream of courage never had.

Kim counts one by one the signs that announce the day, the deep sonorities that separate him from breakfast. The bird first lets out a jarring cry amid the crickets' song. Like an arrow gliding through freshwater. It begins. The neighbor's *chien fer* sets off well before the roosters:* that's when she turns on her bedside lamp and sets her

* *Chien fer* means "iron dog," a short-haired dog endemic to Central America.

radio dial to the Saint-Pierre broadcast. If Kim focuses, if he stops breathing, he can clearly recognize Gospel verses recited by a singer.

"My heart beats fast."

People wake up before the animals, here. They stretch their steps on humid leaves. There, under the mango tree, a man walks toward the house. And the rooster sings, but without much ardor. If the moon is full, Kim can see the shadow of the plum tree dancing on the blinds. It sketches landscapes and monsters, depending on the seasons. A door creaks. Closes. Silence. Kim takes in some air. It smells of dew and grass, humid and fresh. He welcomes this dampness, which soothes the sweat that pierces his temples.

His heart beats fast in the blue hour of the before-daylight when Kim perceives the dull sound of his father smothering the body of his sister in her childhood bed.

To Be a Monster

IT'S KIM.

The neighborhood women are sure of it. They say:

It's Kim, the abomination, the pervert, the monster, the scumbag, the degenerate, the slut, the whore who surely sells her pussy for cheap on the steps of the old courthouse. It's Kim. What else could you expect from a girl like that? God didn't say that. God didn't say you could choose your sex. It's Kim. Her mother had a daughter and the devil slipped into her body, and first of all, it's well-known, everybody knows that family takes their orders directly from Satan, *sé djab selman ki ka koumandé yo.*

When Kim was a child, my neighbor Georgette told everyone that she saw him desecrate the church of Vauclin by wearing ratty boy undergarments under his dress. It's Kim, everybody knows he is a monster, and even his mother knew. The market vendor says: "A nice woman, her mother. She used to work at the bank in Rivière Pilote. A good pious woman."

Georgette says: "*Tjip! Zot pa konnet ayen. Zot pa konnet sé moun-lan.* You mustn't trust people's fineries at church, no. Truth is concealed, only God knows the truth. And the truth is that all the girls in that family serve the devil. Kim's grandmother was a *kimbwaseuse*. She killed her own husband. Kim's the devil's granddaughter. Everybody knows that."

The vendor frowns: "You mustn't illspeak of the dead."

The neighbor smiles: "Those people never die. Those people are *engagés*."

The tone escalates. A crowd gathers around the two shouting women. Men try to talk, but they're sent packing. The matter is too important. "Who are you to judge that woman? To spit on her ancestors?" Georgette stands straight on her spine, she tilts her chin up, and her gaze rips through the saggy body of her interlocutor. "I know things," she hisses. "Those people are *engagés*. They are not dead. Since the time of Guinea, these women have conspired with the devil against Christ. Two whole centuries of demons, that's what this family wrought. I know the whole story! The priest is the one who warned me. And Kim, that thing we call Kim, it's not a killer, it's the devil in the flesh. Instead of calling the cops, we'd all better find her and burn her so that her body can never be reborn. That child is a curse, you hear? The moon mustn't rise upon her living body. Mark my word, with the saints as my witnesses, Kim must die tonight. We must avenge those she killed, and we must avenge God for the blight of her very existence."

To Live Free or Die

"YOUR NEIGHBORS ARE SUCH GASBAGS!"

In Régale, Kim busies himself with barricading the windows, just in case.

"They've been awake for a while, no time to fuck or let the sun rise, they're already on the move. They work in the city, don't they? Ugh, those discount *Nègres* who break their backs for the *béké* make me want to puke. They're all the same. Sheep. What did the poet use to say? She-goats. That's right, a good old herd of she-goats that fights for an octopus or something like that. Isn't that how it goes? *Mè si*, that's it. Well, I can't remember. Bah, I don't know it by heart, but let's be real: no one does, and no one understands and . . . Huh . . . check out those shiny little *chabins*, those golden-skinned shit kickers. They can't be more than ten years of age, they don't have a job, but they're already wearing Lacoste fits. Check 'em out with their golden hair and their golden scratch sneakers! Ah, little shit kickers! Those damn 40 percent freeloaders! GO EAT AN OCTOPUS ALL OF YOU! Yeah, that's right!"

The neighbors cock their ears. Kim freezes. They slam a door and push their kids out of the house. Kim breathes.

"I don't give a damn if they hear me. For real. I don't care. They'll find me either way. Babylon will find me. Whitey knows just how. They're real good at finding stuff. Vaccination America the atomic bomb. Yeah, they found plenty of stuff, and they'll find me too. They'll find me. When I left that cursed *kaz* yesterday, I was covered in blood. I didn't hide. Everyone saw my waxy mug, my eye piercing, my hands . . . There's no one like me. Sooner or later, they will catch me in their net. I don't need to hide, I won't hide. Hiding left my life long ago. They'll find me. So, your neighbors' kids wear a uniform? What the hell is that about? Rich kids need uniforms now? They need to be trained to dress? No. What makes them think our children need uniforms? And they're proud of it, too! And there she goes, the pimped-up mother, the impeccable neighbor who shines her son's egghead. Yeah, alright, you dumb bitch, your kid looks great. No hair, white tee blue jeans no jewelry no braids no rings no tattoos. He is perfect. He is perfectly White. What? You have a problem with what I'm saying? I didn't ask for your two cents, you old hag. Shit. I say what I want. I'm drunk. Do I need permission to speak when I'm drunk? No? Good. I know what I'm saying. I know what I'm talking about. I once worked for the *béké*, you know. Some of us didn't get the memo that slavery was over. No joke! We gotta stop lying to ourselves. *Békés* aren't even the worst. No. The worst are those *Nègres* who employ *Nègres* and work them like slaves. That's to say for nothing. So, for me, *béké* isn't a skin color. I said they work for *békés*, I didn't say they work for Whitey, so don't come tell me I am a racist, no, *mwen pa rasis pies, pa vini di mwen ni rasism kont blan!* I don't give a damn if they're White. There are people in this country who think slavery isn't over. Me, I'm a slave for no one, nothing, no one. I don't work for those people. So I don't work. So I don't work."

Why work? Kim asked himself that question every morning for five years while putting on his proletarian costume. Why work? Kim never imagined that by taking action he could find his own freedom. He never understood that it was the production of wealth that made the world go round and that one had to dedicate oneself to it to change the dance. He never figured out how to place the power of his anger into the correct gear of history. He never figured out he had that power. It would have taken ten years of school lessons and morning sermons to make him understand. Songs and images that look like him in his childhood books, stories on the small screen that told him of the grandeur of his people, and also their lushness, their joys, their search for happiness. And it wasn't for lack of singing tales at home, with Maman, of glorifying memories and beating the *ka*-drums every season. What Kim lacked was enough love to believe in all of it. Love of himself, love of his people for themselves and each other, love that spills into the streets to show the children that together nothing is impossible, that everything is theirs for the taking, that no man, however powerful he may be, should ever have the right to stand in the way of their dreams of greatness. And everything he had ever lacked resounds in his anger that morning, in a rage that steps on its own feet in a tortuous labyrinth of scattered ideas stolen here and there at the whims of encounters and chance. Why work if we don't even know why we're here?

"Laurent, I tell you, I sure saw the cash flow in that soda factory. But I don't even have 100 euros to show for it. I didn't buy a car, travel, invest . . . I didn't do the things adults do, I was there at twenty-three, stuck like a kid at the school-age stage. Like a kid, I just moved when told to. I lifted the arm they told me to lift, and then I lowered the foot they told me to lower. And I paid for my grub, my bus, and because the bus was often late or on strike, I lost days of pay. And then I paid my rent. And then I partied, but partying only keeps us asleep, quiet, so we can go back to work the next day. Yeah, I partied. *Man téadan tout kannaval, tout konsè bod lanmè, tout sound system, tout swaré toutouni asou plaj lisid.* You name it, I was there. I drank what? Their rum, their sodas, their beers, their limes . . . who are they? The same profiteers!! *Sé menn bétjé-a ek sé menm nèg betjé-a! Békés* and Black *békés*, all the same. My minimum wage always went back to the sender. Slavery isn't over, I was just on a fucking plantation, giving my pay to the bookkeeper just before Sunday mass. Amen!

"But I fucked up one day. And so I was fired. Just like that. Easy. And you know what? That day, I didn't shut up. Well. I am free now."

I notice someone new in the shadows. It's a woman sitting on the shore of the in-between-worlds. I recognize the shape of a mango on the dimple of her right cheek. It's Sidonie, our grandmother, who looks on as the contents of Kim's stomach spill out. Alive, she, too, had gotten drunk after killing someone. But that one, that husband that only talked with his fists, he had deserved to get killed. "Why is this boy in so much pain?" she wonders, nodding softly. "What happened?" Flooded with sadness, the ghost cocks her gauzy head to the side and tries to sense the soul of her descendant. And I can't talk to her. And so I tuck away my own distress inside a soap bubble, and I hang on to my desire to take her in my arms to comfort her and tell her: It's not your fault. It's the world that led your grandson astray by crushing him under the weight of lies and myths in which he was an aberration. The child doesn't see us tremble, and his cries drown Sidonie's sobs:

"You think it's over? That's what you think, Laurent? You think Papa Césaire fixed everything, don't you? You believe that, yeah, you do, you're a good guy, you're a good guy, you gotta respect the dead. You're right me too I am gonna respect the dead. I'm gonna. But for now, life down here is an endless comedy of people taking advantage of others, people trampling others. People who think they're so White that they bless France more than the French themselves! And you too, you swim in that, Laurent! You, your feet are pink from wading in ponds of blood. Don't you dare look at me like I'm a piece of shit. You aren't worth a dime more than me. The worst is that you still believe in it, you still believe you're in France, don't you? I knew it . . . You know how many people are poor here? You ever ventured outside of your fucking *morne* with its bougie villas whose owners have forgotten how to search the ground for yams? Are you sure, are you really sure you're in France? I'll break it down for you, you old fuck. They have us in a chokehold, your Voltaires and your Montesquieus. They have us in a chokehold, and they keep us too poor to live and too rich to protest. They have us. What have you done, you heap of trash, to help us awaken to ourselves? But I know, I know for a fact because I dug around, that some of you, your friends even, were ready to take arms, were ready to take back our freedom. But they couldn't, could they? What can we do, David, squaring off with a nuclear Goliath? France will never let go of the Antilles, Laurent! And Antilleans will never let go of France! And it's not just their cruelty and our cowardice. It's their cowardice and our cruelty, too! Nothing good can ever come out of these unions where one steps on his wife to stand tall. I know how they think, those people who govern us. And I tell you: Never, your dusty ballot boxes your bellowed slogans your assemblies of bigoted old men and your pawnshop-like ministries will never set the system afire. We should have killed, damn it! Because only death scares us enough to force us to rise up in revolt, to force us to resist. It's death that aroused Haiti and gave Delgrès the thirst for freedom! Death only, because protests don't work, posters don't work, general strikes don't work, trials don't work! Here is my trial! A blood bath! Because only blood will atone for blood, and once spilled, you can't ignore blood anymore! It drools on the whole world, scandalous, unbearable, foul! The whole world must rise up for it to stop! And I will be the one who begins the end. My heart beats, Laurent! I am alive my heart beats! Freedom is right here, my heart beats! I will die tonight. I will die free. Live free or die? Freedom is dead, we tried everything, Laurent! It's dead forever. So let's end it, I will kill us tonight, that's it, the only pride we have left! That's what my ancestors would have wanted. I believe it, I do. I think it was to possess their humanity anew that they begged sorcerers for licorice seeds. Today, it is our last freedom, and it is how the world will topple once more! We must end history, Laurent! I will not let another generation of stale *Nègres* like you rise again on my lands!"

Sidonie cocks her head to the side, whistling. She never asked for her children to be so angry. She never asked for them to erect gallows and guillotines. You can't wash blood with blood. The blood spilled on the soil can only thicken the viscous swell that clings to the land since the White man massacred the intractable First Nations in the belly of America. And Sidonie is right. It's such a man thing to think you can cleanse better with a dirty cloth than with a clean sponge. It's such a man thing to think that you can fix something by destroying it. It's such a man thing to want to take from the one who has taken, to want to do unto his flesh what you couldn't prevent him from doing to yours.

Sidonie looks away from her lost son. "He sounds like my mother, Léonide," she moans as she crosses the shores of the in-between-worlds to land on the *kaz*'s patio. And that's where she finds her, Léonide, hanging by her neck from the branch of the kapok tree, her gaze devotedly turned toward the house where the criminal preaches. She swings her liana-like body beneath the branch and exults in a madness that was hers well before death:

"It's you, *Manman*! You're the one who filled the little one's head with these horrors. It's you, you ignorant fury, who made a martyr out of him. You're the one who convinced him to suicide this body for which your mothers had fought so hard. Admit it, you witch!"

"My son!" she whispers with the last filament of air threading through her neck. "My son will save us."

"*Manman* Léonide, we are already dead."

"My son will save more than our lives: our honor! He will save us."

"Selfish! Degenerate! What did you tell him?"

"The truth."

"*Your* truth!"

"The only one there is!"

With her voice, Léonide stills time for the two ancestors to settle their scores.

"The only truth," she goes on. "The only one I know, the only one that resembles it. My truth, Sidonie, will never know rest. My truth didn't drown in the viscid waters that flow under the bridge where the dead roam. My truth remained buried here, in the ground. It rushed between Foyal's cobblestones, carried with my own blood.[2] That truth never dies, daughter of mine. Blood doesn't burn, no, blood doesn't go away. That's why, that's why we did not really die that's why, because we bled too much to cross over."

"But I never bled, *Maman* . . ."

"Hokum! Sidonie! Hokum! And I bled for you before you and all those before you bled more blood than ever coursed through your veins! So even your blood, long before your birth, had already been spilled in the ground there. Never. Never will memory slacken its talons. Never. Some things will never die, like the voice of the man who threw me out on the street when the first Nazi cannons felled France. Some things will never die, like the name of the man who dragged my body all the way to the port. Just as sure as the sun never dies, some things will never die, in truth, like the light of the whorehouse where my body washed up, *an tan Wobè*, between the canal and the cemetery for the rich, between the muck and the glistening cars where people are just so happy, you know, at night.[3] Memory doesn't go away, it returns always, as sure as the sun does in the morning! The blood spilled on my cold sex when the third soldier exited it. Some things just won't die, like the memory of his eyes, when he said: 'Léonide! I want to see your pink sex sing the Marseillaise!' And my sex did sing! It unfurled its guts on the soldier's malodorous mouth while another waited, holding a knife under my throat. Shoot me, soldier! Cleave my neck and get it over with! I said it I said it! I said it, that I preferred death!"

"No. You didn't."

"Then I cut this throat myself and it is my necklace this morning! I killed my head, and no one can take that ultimate freedom from me! The child is right! I defeated those monsters by wrenching my body back from them! It's the only silence that belongs to me! Yes, Sidonie, yes! I told him, I told my great-grandson that our death is the only sacred path toward our freedom!"

"Crazy old hag. Did your death bring an end to your descendants' suffering? Did it succeed in killing the memory? Had you predicted that you would survive death when you killed yourself to forget? How did suicide work out for you? Who did you leave on earth in truth? A dead memory? Or a living daughter?"

"You only think about yourself. I should have raised you better. Your father spoiled you, that's what. Never would I have let you rot, you and your daughter, selling your asses to the colonizers, slipping into their world, trying on their shoes to pretend. I did not flee, you're the ones who fled your own history. Me, I am dead, but I remained proud."

"You're insane. And you are betraying the memory of our mothers by taking the weapons and the path of those they fought bitterly against. The darkness that devoured your body long ago, you are slipping toward it, *Manman. Zafé'w pa ta'y.* Don't drag Kim down with you."

"It's too late, Sidonie. If you want to save him, you have to let me go. Give me a chance. *Ban mwen an ti chans, tianmay . . . An fwa, dé fwa.* Twice thirty-six times. I want to die, Sidonie. I want to die and never exist again. And nothing more under my tomb, nothing. Absence. The void of the opaque and tarry sky and then nothing. *Sa bout!* I cry seventy-two men pounding my body for a coin in and a coin out. For a roof made of silence and a mouthful of land. For a piece of nothing and a basketful of stale bread for me, for my sickly mother, for you who wailed endlessly! Kill me, witch of my blood! Kill me so that I may no longer feel this beating heart! Or I will kill once more, twice more, thirty-six times more! Kill me for good!"

And the Hanged One swings so hard that the skin on her neck might just tear against what's left of her braided rope. The wind rushes between the branches of the kapok tree. Sidonie hesitates to execute her mother's wish. But undoing the spell that Ayo cast to maintain them all on the shores of the world of the living would take everything, leaving her with no power at all. And Sidonie has bigger fish to fry than to relieve *Manman* Léonide's soul. She should use her power to try to reason with Kim. Ah, if she could, if only she could talk to him, Grandma Sidonie. Kim would listen to her. Kim always listened to her. And Kim could tell her, too. She always listened to him when he was a child. If she could cross over into this world and talk to Kim, maybe she could save him. But in this moment of hesitation, Sidonie sees Cédric, my son, her last heir, walking toward the shores of the other world.

He is about to cross. I see him. My Cédric. My child. My darling little boy. How handsome, his body stretching in the shadow, silently. His arms sway with the infinite sweetness of our cuddles after our nightly story. Oh, how I feared this image, and how now, I long to see his face! But he is facing away from me, and I can only see his round skull and the mounts and valleys of the braids I weaved for him a few days before his departure. He takes our art with him. My crowned son, my son, already greater than us, moving fearlessly toward a world we know nothing about.

It's a happy child who is about to cross. He looks like Sidonie. He has her sweet way of tilting her head when she thinks. But not at this hour. Between worlds, his body, weighed down, doesn't hesitate as it moves toward the kapok tree, tree of life, tree of death, the sentinels' gate. So Sidonie feels that there is more love beyond the shore, near Cédric, than on this tortured earth. She closes her eyes on the world of the living, and catching a glimpse of another world beyond the breach, she seizes her chance, abandons Kim, breaks Ayo's spell for herself and flees with the child toward the elsewhere, without a single look back.

I never imagined that my grandmother was such a coward. We're only disappointed by the people we love.

To Kill the Child Who Did Nothing

IN THE *KAZ*, KIM IS HUNGRY. Now that the alcohol is waning in his veins, his organs remind him that he hasn't swallowed anything solid since the previous morning. But Kim is a picky eater. As children, we ate everything. Anyway, we didn't have the option to snub Maman's food. We never worried about its nutritional value or its composition. It tasted of love, and that was more than enough. However, over the last few years, Kim has become militant. He only eats local food. Laurent's kitchen, full of plastics and half-empty containers, would have ruined his appetite if his guts hadn't threatened to purge their bile until blood through his coarse throat. So, for an instant, he suspends his disgust and opens the fridge. The truce doesn't last long:

"Laurent, Laurent! You don't know how to shop, do you? Your reserves are more rotten than your brain. There's nothing good in there, man! You gotta stop subsidizing assholes, you know? Your milk? You don't even know where it's from. Your potatoes? Chlordeconed.[4] Your packaged meat? Food for dogs that they sell to *Nègres* instead of burning it. *Tou sa lajan ou ka genyen!* What's the point in being rich only to buy Europe's garbage? Alright. We're celebrating me today. I'll take some President butter and smooth it over organic toast."

For an instant, Kim remembers his kitchen, which he left impeccably clean the previous morning before packing his things and leaving his one-bedroom apartment in Fort-de-France. There, he left a jar of homemade guava jam that would have given this toast the caress the skin of his lips now craves. He should have finished that jar of jam and taken its smell with him all the way to hell.

Kim butters two more toasts for Laurent and joins him on the sofa. The sun is already poking through the mist. The day is coming. The world covers the kapok tree with a golden powder.

As he crunches on his dry toast, Kim plays in his head a slow music that covers the world, waiting for his cue. He closes his eyes and follows the silken steps of each morsel from his mouth to his stomach. He feels the gratitude of his flesh all along his neck and in his stomach, impatience, a feeling he knows so well. And when the sustenance reaches its destination, the pleasure, delectable, fills and lulls him. He sinks into the sofa and stops chewing. He feels on his eyelids the sun pushing through the barricades. His heart beats fast, and he stops breathing.

It's always like that. It will never change. In the morning, when the mist lifts and the frogs hush, Kim becomes a child again in a cloud of lies, still, until the sun imposes life upon this strange parenthesis where the world must escape. Will each morning always be like this, until his dying day, waiting for his throat to loosen just enough to let some air through? Kim has been holding his breath for nearly twenty years now. He has been holding his breath since the days when, to do nothing, he pretended to be asleep. He holds his breath to refrain from screaming, to not anger Maman, to not kill her. So that Maman doesn't kill his father. He holds his breath to let his father rape me every morning and so that he can do nothing about it.

Kim has never seen the beautiful dawn in Martinique. He has never seen darkness recede under the cupola, and the stars dim with the frogs' song. He knows nothing of the absolute tenderness with which blue turns to pink on the horizon before imposing itself anew over the orange troubles that striate the clouds. And Kim's skin, overcome with chills, doesn't know how the morning caresses the flesh and softens the eyelids. Kim's skin doesn't know if dawn could ever place, in the hollow of his heart, the sweet pearls of the happy days that our land once bore.

Forever, on Kim's skin, the sun's rays are a blinding beam, a bone-chilling shower, a stretched silence. No remedy could ever give him his mornings nor mine back. Nor Maman's.

Tonight, Kim will be between four walls. Where they will imprison him, he won't see the sky, he won't see the sun. The day will no longer rise. Maybe then, Kim will be able to breathe dawn in for the first time. He imagines his ordeal behind bars. He is not like his ancestor Léonide. He doesn't really want to kill himself. He wants a trial to speak, to speak for the first time, a trial to say everything and a bedroom with no windows. And while he waits for the night he longs for, daylight comes, terrifying.

"Don't worry, sister," he whispers for me. "I am here, and now, you have nothing to fear. You will take your cell phone, you will see your messages. Don't panic, Édith, it's me. I love you, my dear sister, and everything will be ok."

Oh, brother of mine, how I hate you.

Kim shivers, as if he had heard me. He imagines, in truth, my bloodshot face, he leaps out of his world to project himself into the stormy heart of his big sister when she finds out he killed her son.

"Don't look at me like that!" Kim yells at Laurent, ragingly hurling a large cabinet to the floor. The old china that was gathering dust in it bursts into dismembered crumbs on the white tile. Kim nearly falls over stepping on the disaster, still drunk, still lost. His thoughts become blurry. His naked feet are bloody. He stumbles forward, dives toward the sofa and jams his knife against the wide chest of his hostage. His breath fogs up Laurent's bifocal lenses. He trembles. Then he takes a step back, panting, looking at him.

Kim turns his back to dawn and, screaming, looks for a lifeline on the walls to help pull his head out of the memory sludge where he is drowning.

Outside, it's raining.

As the sun rises in Régale, its rays gild the rain's droplets. The sky gives Kim a cool respite before the turmoil, like a pressure cooker, ensnares him into a sticky lukewarm haze. "Soon, we'll sweat like fresh cadavers. Cold skin but blood still warm. My neck is already clammy. It's the alcohol. Alcohol sets you on fire." Kim wrings his soaked shirt and lets his chest breathe in the dawn.

There, on his half-nude body, his sweat follows curves that no longer belong to him. And yet he looks for his body, longs to return to it, to the time when in childhood he could still exist, to the time before Laurent, his father, crushed my sex. He wants to discover that virile body anew, the one he could sense as a child when he closed his eyes, he wants to become his mother's son once more and cease to be the son of a rapist. But when he closes his eyes, Kim only sees the paralyzed child, the child who did nothing. And killing Cédric changed nothing. And the alcohol too failed to dissolve the vile beast that took up residence in his chest. The monster is still there. So still gripping the knife, Kim looks at Laurent and smiles, for he has in his hands the life he must pluck to salvage his own.

Régale

"I did not forget my wound. I left it on the edges of the world. We all do this, that's how we women survive. I took my body, I brought it to the threshold of death, and I left it there, near the ones my ancestors had left before me. And then the Breaths brought me back to life and ever since, I've been surviving."

EXCERPT OF A LETTER FROM ÉDITH TO HER BROTHER

To Inherit a Legacy

ON A SUMMER AFTERNOON, on the terrace of the Régale home, Maman is braiding my hair. She hums a wordless tune that intrigues her girlfriend but Kim knows it. Kim recites it silently, pensive, waiting for his turn. He must be no more than seven, and, stuck in this so-called girl's body, which he understands very little about, he endlessly looks for Maman's hands, her skin, warm and dense, the fleshy tips of her fingers whose touch gives him an idea of his own density. For now, Maman's magic fingers fly around my skull with fascinating celerity.

Me, I'm staring at a planter overflowing with bougainvillea with the eyes of a *manicou*-possum. I hear neither Maman's songs nor her incantations. I am sitting between her legs, with my back very straight, with my arms around my restless knees. I am not like Kim. I hate getting my hair braided. It hurts. Those hands, always on my skull, hurt me. I often beg, with loud cries, to have my hair relaxed like all my friends in middle school whose smooth locks have never known pain, or so it seems, and Maman has nothing but harsh words for the parents of those children, swearing with a *tjip* flooded with contempt that while she's alive, no one will put lye on her daughters' skulls. So I keep my beautiful mane of *grennen*-coils, and Maman tends to it. Maman parts it, combs it, twists it between her fingers and turns it into works of art. Kim looks at me, suffering under my crown, annoyed. How dare I complain surrounded by servants?

Across from me, sitting in a hammock made of thick canvas, Marraine swings softly and squints, serious, as she listens to Maman regale her with a *milan*-gossip. Marraine approves and reproves in unison with a movement of her lips, at just the right times. Marraine is an old friend of Maman's, close enough to treat us as her own children, too far to know our most intimate secrets. She is a *debouya*-resourceful woman, the kind who has never seen a real paycheck but who has worked every job. Over the course of her eclectic career path, she bore witness to all sorts of people, to all sorts of rickety homes, to all sorts of mosaic families, to all sorts of shady dealings *an ba fey*. I love listening to her tell the story of our *tout-monde*-whole-world. It's a nice break from the ghosts spells and nightmares Maman sketches daily. She is Kim's *marraine*-godmother, but she is generous enough to coddle us both. Mine, a plane took her to France one day, and she never came back.

Maman catches the little hairs near my ear, pulls them and I let out a small, shrill cry, reaching for my roots lest she pull them out completely. Maman has not a care for my implorations. She braids in mere seconds an arabesque on my skull and covers my voice by speaking to Marraine about the inheritance. Kim doesn't listen to any of it. He had never wanted to know anything about indivision. But me, I am interested. I stop whining, and I ask.

I ask who built the house, the house where the three of us live. "None of your business," Kim hisses between his teeth. "It's your great-grandmother Léonide who lived here first," Maman replies. "She had a *kaz* on this plot, right where my bedroom is."

And then I have the urge to ask who she was, that great-grandmother, what she did and with whom . . . it's effective: Maman lets go of my hair to tell the story. I sigh, relieved.

Marraine says: "Marie-Magdeleine, the mother of your poor Léonide, was the neighbor of my great-grandmother. She was a binder on a sugarcane plantation at the time when the rum distilleries were running at full steam in the south. World War I made White people thirsty! So, during those years, everybody was breaking their back in the fields. *Tout neg té ka ralé kann.* It wasn't slavery, no, but it was hard. But Marie-Magdeleine was lucky. One day, a White man who was riding through the plantation fell in love with her, *flègèdè*-crash-boom. They had a child. That was your great-grandmother, Léonide. Because Marie-Magdeleine was poor, the man's family decided to raise Léonide near the city, and that was good for her! So Léonide went to school."

Maman says: "That's true, but Léonide couldn't stay in the city when she grew older. And when she returned to this neighborhood, it was complicated . . . her peers were Black, real Black, and jealous. *Épi an tan Wobè*, during the Second World War, with the scarcity, there wasn't enough food for everybody, so . . ."

Marraine quickly jumps back in: "So Léonide went back to the city. She found work with French soldiers. When the war was over, a soldier seduced her, he was Martinican, okay?, so not a collaborator. Your grandmother Sidonie was born, and they came back to live in Régale in the fifties." Kim, who drinks the words of adults like one watches soap operas on TV, is suddenly yanked from his reverie by a cacophony of voices howling in French, in Kreyol, voices from the other world that burst loud enough to be heard by the living. They yell:

"Shame on these two *makrels*! How dare they feed these lies to these children?" "*Sé sa yo té pou ba ich'lan, sa yo té lé matché an venn-li, sé sa yo té pé lésé an fondok fal ti manmay-lan!*" "Drink! Let's drink the sweet nectar of a life of *self-made poto mitan.*[5] Let's sprinkle some talcum on their chocolate behinds, we have a White ancestor my friends, a nice one, a good one, a lover! Yes, ma'am!"

"Hokum!" "*Bann ipocrit . . .*" "*A pa zot ki té ka valé tout grenn a zozio a!*" "*Asé di! Sé ti manmay-lan péké jan séré an listwa bèkèkè kon tala.*" "You hypocrites! How will your children ever know their history?" "Love? *Tip!*" "*An lélékou yo ka krié lanmou!*" "A nightmare you call love!" "Jesus Mary Joseph pray for them, they know not what they are doing . . ." "*Ladjé sé fanmi sent la épi ba on ti wouspel pou yo pé soukoué tjou yo an ba la tè, sakré malfini!*" "Leave the saints alone, and let's teach them a lesson!"

Kim stands up, turns his head, looks for the voices. Maman stares at her youngest daughter with concern. She stands up, too, and puts a reassuring hand on Kim's shoulder.

Maman's hand. The skin, once more. The body recovered. Kim no longer hears the voices. Kim returns to Maman's world, Maman who loves him, who smiles at him. The world where the women of his family climbed life's ladder armed with nothing but courage, pride, and love. Love. That's what Maman gives Kim. Kim listens, and sits back down.

Later that night, during one of those self-induced insomnias during which Kim willed himself awake in hopes of being sound asleep in the morning, the ghosts' quarrel rocks the borders of the worlds so hard that Kim sits up in his bed to hear them better. He then begins, alone, the journey I learned to make after countless lessons with Maman. He doesn't do it well, so it takes him several tries, and when finally he perceives the voices, he holds on to them and keeps them close to his soul as a rampart against the morning demons.

<<< >>>

Since then, the voices have never left Kim, but he never succeeds in talking to them. Kim loves this troubled company that gets worked up in his consciousness from time to time. And that's how Ayo's daughters unwittingly accompanied my brother all throughout his adolescence.

I didn't know that Kim could hear our ancestors. We never talked about it. I know them, too, and I know them better than he does. And it's because I know them, because I was told about them, and because I listened, that I am not crazy today.

The most talkative of them all is Célestine. She grew up in Régale, after the definitive abolition of slavery, where she cultivated medicinal plants.[6] She had learned that science from her father, Ayo's son, and from the maroons who had raised him, in the *mornes'* heights. With him, Célestine pushed further into the forest than Ayo ever did during her lifetime. So Célestine knew each shoot of this land, each mineral, each stream, and each scent. We don't know how her father died, but it's at his side that Ayo found Célestine in the Régale woods in 1855. And it's to her that Ayo spoke from the in-between-worlds for the first time. Célestine is the first descendant to have been initiated by the ghost. Of Célestine, Maman would say that by learning Kongo magic from Ayo and by marrying it to the science of the earth inherited from the Kalinagos and the maroons, she had become the most powerful healer of all the Antilles. People consulted her from far away, whether by written words or by magic, to devise rituals, anoint sanctuaries, heal death, and snuff life. She was the ancestral temple that the Whites wanted to take away from us, the memory of our healing trances and of our encounters. But with age, the fear of death and its decrees had made Célestine shroud her miracles in silence, a silence colonized by her litanies and supplications to a God she had never seen. With her whispering in his ears, Kim learned almost the entire Gospel: all of Célestine's beyond-the-grave interventions inevitably end with a mention of the sacred text, immediately followed by a unanimous *tjip* from all of her own descendants.

Marie-Magdeleine, so-called fortunate after having been fucked by a plantation bookkeeper during the Great War, is the first to blaspheme after her own mother's Christian effusions. She is also the best beguine singer and an insatiable gossiper when it comes to the romantic life of the city. But the fiercest has always been Léonide, Marie-Magdeleine's daughter. A whore for the French soldiers during World War II, Léonide hates half of the planet, the half with sagging balls, and among that half, she hates the ones with pale skin with a little more gusto. Mulattoes are not far behind, and neither are *Nègres*, for their complicit silence. She became an expert in curses, powerful enough, it seems, to pierce the guardrail that protects the living from the irascible ire of the dead.

However, never has Kim heard Ayo in his dreams, even though the ghosts spoke of her often, nor has he ever heard Sidonie because he knew her alive.

When he is fourteen, Maman goes to see Kim in the garden and asks him if he wants to speak to Ayo. He pretends he doesn't understand. Maman doesn't insist. She thinks that the spell of the Kongo witch is growing weaker still and rejoices. The witch had promised Ayo that none of her children would be born into slavery. She kept her word: Ayo bore one son of whom we know nothing but that he died a maroon. Her descendants each bore one daughter at a time, heiress to Ayo's magic. Because the gift depleted all uterine energy, never had this lineage produced siblings. Maman was the first to have two babies she had desired. It's the proof, she thinks, that the spell is waning. She never imagined that it was proof that it grew stronger. She never thought she had transmitted the magic twice. On the contrary, she thinks that her little Kim is saved and that I, her daughter Édith, absorbed it all when I was born. She thinks it isn't necessary to impose the initiation on two children. But Maman still asks if Kim hears the Breaths. His silence confirms her theory. So she applies a tender kiss to her daughter's forehead and walks away, serene, with her history and her secrets. Maman walks away, but Léonide, who witnessed the scene from afar, understands that Kim didn't tell his mother the truth. So Léonide swoops down on the child, pushes the door left ajar in his consciousness and enters. She takes her quarters in the child's starved spirit. She nests there in the absence of an answer from Maman. And over the course of the days, months, years that follow that missed encounter in the garden, Léonide patiently cultivates hatred in Kim's heart. Hatred is a simple response to complicated questions. Hatred is an easy path to follow for those who have been abandoned in the labyrinth of a false history. Hatred is what Léonide gives to Kim as a sweet treat when he hungers for knowledge. When Kim thirsts for words, Léonide shows him images of his foremothers gagged tortured dying, hanging from the branches of the kapok tree. When he thirsts for courage, she tells him of the runaway spirits turned mad in the forest, with hounds on their trail. When he thirsts for meaning, she pours down his throat the blood spilled by his ancestors so that he could exist. So Kim thirsts for blood. And since Maman stays quiet, since Maman offers nothing else of interest, Kim calls Léonide whenever he is thirsty, so that she may give him more blood still. And she has a lot, a lot of it to offer.

To Summon a Hurricane

STORM WARNING ON *morne* Régale, water seeps into Maman's house between the joints eroded by time. It gnaws at the wrinkly coating under the decrepit sheet of corrugated iron and the drops of water beat on the roof at a ceaseless cadence. *La pli si tol* is no longer a love song: it's a machine gun. It pulled the entire family out of bed, a scattered group of humans that coalesces into a tribe when trouble is afoot.

The night won't hush up. It imposes its terrible discourse on the world. The thunderstorm rumbles far away, over there, where the world is awakening. The house's lights, still bright, run from the bedroom to the living room to obstruct the rivulets that pool between the tiles. The children play in the puddles near the TV and scream at every clap of thunder.

The deafening concert of the sky's waters stifles the screams of the devastated neighborhood. You can't help people you can't hear. And then the house sinks. And then the house is in a hurry. The race against time exhausts the grown-ups. Tirelessly, they mop up the dirty ponds that damage the expensive furniture in the living room. They salvage what they can: photos books hard drives clothes DVDs the console. They bring down to the ground the demijohn in which the Christmas shrub used to macerate when Grandma Sidonie was still there, when she told stories of hurricanes past and of the lives they blew away. They remove her photos from the rain and under the doors they pile up her lace sheets, her madras petticoats corsets shawls to bind her hips; they throw everything to the ground, which rumbles and squeaks under the thunder. In her room, Maman obsessively dries an African mural painted on her wall. She is afraid it will be erased. I help her: It's the door to the shore of the in-between-worlds.

The child screams. The thunderstorm awakens him. His sisters and cousins dance around his crib. The parents get mad. Everybody runs and yells, some jokingly, others to restore order. Be quiet, you insolent brood, sit down in a corner and stay there, sit down I said, *pé!* Let the storm pass.

The tropical storm comes back nearly every year. It makes the walls tremble and the stagnant waters boil up to the surface. In the middle of the night, it brings hordes of tarantulas into the house. They terrify the adults and fascinate the children. And when the power goes out and we light up candles to watch time go by the way it used to, the grown-ups, pacified, tell the children the frightening stories of much scarier days when the storm turned into a hurricane. So, the children dream of a hurricane.

And their hearts beat fast.

Maman sings in the kitchen. She is preparing a fete of extraordinary insanity. I recognize the day she threw our father out for good.

Kim is fifteen, I think, and I am taking my high school exit exam, and all of our friends put together couldn't possibly match Maman's girlfriends in number and in clamor. DJ, amuse-bouches, BBQ, lasers, disco ball, the foremothers' furniture is pushed to the edge of the living-room-turned-dancefloor, and on the patio, there are domino tables, an open bar, card games, and loud boozy debates about politics, anti-colonialism, and recipes for poppy flower shampoo. Much too tightly squeezed in a low-rise pair of jeans and a laced-up top that accentuates the fullness of her breasts and belly, Maman floats between her dancers and her guests, speaking loudly and governing the whole earth. The grown-ups listen to Perle Lama, dance to Kassav', and launch into mazurkas and the teens vainly try to exist by besieging the dance floor during zouk songs with a simulacrum of sensuality that makes quadragenarian singles laugh during national holidays.

Kim and I celebrate all night, all week, all year. We keep the date written in the calendar. When I move out to study at the university's Schœlcher campus, Kim calls me on the phone every year on April 22 to reminisce about that party, that ending, that beginning, without ever uttering what it had been the end of. We remain in silence just for a moment, leaving room for the dead to breathe. And then, since I sense the ripping apart of his body, since he brings me back to the ripping apart of mine, since I couldn't sew his rip back together, since it wasn't my job to do so, I whisper in Kim's impatient ear, to make him alive again: "For it is in the roots of your black hair that all the power rests. For it is the whirlwind of your dark curls that ciphers our secret. For it is in the storm of your rising locks that the seal of our silence will break."

To Return from Exile

KIM PASSES HIS EXIT EXAM. And he is put on a plane. No one asked him. No one proposed it to him. It's how it is. It is written somewhere that it must be so. Kim passes his exit exam and steps onto a plane full of people like him who passed their exit exam. These young adults dreamed of leaving, to stop rotting away in this shithole. Nothing can hold them back, like a pack of voracious dogs left starving for months and released on the same day upon the carcass of a Charolais bull.

When we were little girls, Maman would tell her friends:

"There's no work here, why would Édith and Kim stay in Martinique? To trifle in the streets waiting for their next temp job? No! There's no work here, and don't talk to me about the university. *Tjip!* A daycare, *an lékol volèz*, a ripoff. I didn't feed these girls for them to vegetate here."

Me, I marooned after the exit exam. I stayed.

But Kim swallows everything Maman says just like Célestine drinks the Gospel's word. He doesn't even think about doing anything else. So with his open-sesame-exit-exam in the bag, before hopping on the plane, Kim and his friends drink the life of Martinican youths in one single gulp since no one will let them leisurely sip at the bottle. One month to check out all the skiffs, fuck on a boat, fuck for the first time, get drunk, or pretend, go out clubbing, at all the clubs, until all the money gifted by Marraine to settle in the magic country is up in a smoke of alcohol and frenzy. It's Célestine's Breath that looms over the Dionysian hours of her descendant. She disapproves loudly, all the while watching. Marie-Magdeleine, on the other hand, rhythmically applauds the best life of this being, emancipated from the useless sermons of old fanatical misogynists like her mother. The foremothers' bickering makes Kim roar with laughter in the midst of his pleasure.

It's during those rambling nights that Kim cast away the verb and found his own language, but he never told me the details of it. Léonide's mother can't help but drag me to this initial day, to help me unravel the knots of my brother's silences. So I find Kim and his friends hurtling down a cliff of northern Martinique in evening wear. Their laughter explodes with cries of victory, howls of hope, and roars of glory. Having escaped a smoky concert and landed on a black-sand beach, the children shed their societal garb on the shore and rush into the sea, naked. Kim runs ahead and dives into the silent depths, where the world quiets down. His body floats, dissolves, disappears, and instead of his skin, the current outlines the contours of his soul. Kim drowns along with his legacy. Kim drowns far away from his childhood, from his mornings, from the rapes, from the lies and the silences. The salty water seeps into his lungs and invades his veins until it devours the past.

There, under the celestial and gray auspices, choking on the waters of a new baptism with his chosen brothers, Kim emerges from the sea and vomits his own name. The world now splits in front of his narrowed eyes. Somewhere far, drums beat to the rhythm of his heart. Kim leaves his friends who squabble playfully in the sea foam. He runs on the sand. But out of the water, his skin hounds him, his sex drips and his breasts bounce against his body. So he screams, and he pulls at them as hard as he can, convinced that all he has to do is rip them off! His bruised skin resists, and he is still pulling when Marie-Magdeleine screams: "Stop! My son!"

He stops.

"Kim. I know you can hear me. Come on, young man, get up! We're going home." Kim blinks as he catches his breath. It's not the voice of a ghost he hears, perhaps it's the alcohol tricking him. His friends are there, they put their arms around his shoulders, and standing in front of him our neighbor, Sébastien, grabs his hand. "You're a man, Kim, stop fucking around. You don't have anything to prove to anybody."

In the beyond, Célestine sings her Ave Marias and her sisters cheer with salt water to Kim's health.

With their clubbing money gone, August drags on. Kim and his mates hitchhike. Going to the beach is an endless expedition that widens the abyss of their resentment. Between two trips sitting in the back of generous pickup trucks, the five friends spit their rage on the asphalt, their rage at being here, their anger toward those useless politicians who can't get it together to build a decent bus system, toward that band of subsidized parasites who suck their mothers' taxes dry to build swimming pools but can't manage to bring water to everyone's tap. There on the scorching side of the road, these young men swear that they will never, never come back to this rock where you'll die a slow painful death before seeing a bus go by, where you waste your salary on fare tickets every month for the luxury of going to study things that are neither useful nor lucrative in an empty university. If you hitchhike, you have to wake up at 6:00 A.M. to get to Salines Beach before noon. That gives you time to talk. Sitting on concrete ruins, waiting for a car to go by, Kim shares with his friends stupid questions to pass the time. The Breaths make me witness this moment when Kim asks his brothers-in-arms:

"At the end of the day, what does it mean to be a boy?"

"Come on, man," Sébastien sighs. "Not again."

"No, no, seriously, guys. Me, I had to ask myself, but you, you don't have my history, so what is it for you? A piece of flesh that dangles between your thighs?"

"Pff, no man," Sébastien replies, shoving him. "To be a guy is more than that. There are people who have balls and who aren't half a man."

"That's right!" one of our cousins approves.

"A real man, you recognize him when you see him in the street."

"And what's he look like?"

Silence. Kim waits. His friend squints and says:

"A real man's got a blade."

And Sébastien takes it out of his pocket. Kim's heart jumps out of his chest.

"Maybe you never know you're a man," Sébastien says. "But you're sure you're a man when you knifed someone. And you didn't get caught."

The kids gauge each other, in a terrible hesitation. Nobody says anything. Someone will have to break the silence. The cousin slaps Kim in the back as he gets up to flag down a pickup truck and throws out, laughing: "Hey, Sébastien, if you don't get caught, no one will ever know you're a real man, *sakré makoumè!*"

The gang bursts into insults, and Kim follows, pensive. At the end of his reverie, he lands on this beach, with a volleyball, a bottle of coconut water, and a bathing suit. The young men stop horsing around. They look at the sea.

In the calm and supple blue, seaweeds stretch their limbs. They bring to the land of the living the Breaths of those who drowned at sea. The drowned are millions strong. Their bones fell to the depths of the abyss, where another life swallows the leftovers of our world. The submerged volcanoes digested these bodies' calcium and reduced it to powder. At last, the currents brought it here.

Tuning into the echo of a faraway wail, Kim drops in front of the sea and tries to understand. Sand squeaks under his knees and pierces his skin. His hands burrow into the embers, and he lifts the world, which trickles away one grain at a time. Dry. In the rustling of the sand, Kim hears Breaths he doesn't understand. He doesn't speak their language. He doesn't really know how to hear them. Yet those souls are screaming between the hands of the reluctant sorcerer. And when the last grain escapes his fingers, Kim gets up from the froth and leaves. And from then on, the land silently holds the residue of the stateless children forsaken on the beach.

Kim and his friends could have realized during this vacation that, all things considered, life in Martinique wasn't so bad. They see other young adults on the beach, the ones who have money and a car. They look fresh. One day, Kim's eyes fall on round shoulders, swaying under a Caribbean almond tree. He follows their curves, and his eyes glide on nimble arms. These arms are dishing out a meal of Colombo to a slew of children and old-timers, while hips are swinging to a timeless Kassav' tune. Kim moves his own hips in rhythm with this being that calls out to him, unknowingly, and details the dunes and valleys of this back pearling with sweat, which he would have loved to explore. He would have loved to stay and dance.

That day, on the way back, Kim has a doubt. A weight, a pang, his blood won't flow. On the beach, was it the dead he had felt coming out of the sand to grab his ankles and anchor him to the land of his foremothers? But he is not awakened enough to the Breaths to have noticed them. Misreading his doubt, he keeps for himself the music the sea the Colombo the sensual promise and the children's laughter like a secret. And he packs up his bags.

<<< >>>

The morning of his departure, before taking the plane, Kim goes downtown with Marraine. Marraine is his mother through hard times and important days. Since Kim's childhood, she insists on giving him, to Maman's great chagrin, candy from France, Barbie dolls, and soppy novels. Sometimes, as a joke, Maman says she should have given the role of *marraine*-godmother to one of her cousins instead of running the risk of entrusting her daughters to someone who clearly doesn't share her values. So Marraine roars with laughter and hugs Maman. In truth, Maman knows that friendship is worth more than blood and that no tie in life gives more to a woman than the one that binds her to her best friend. And despite all the love and complicity between those two women, and despite all the faith that Kim has in that woman, Marraine doesn't know the serious things. That's why Kim loves her, for those docile days spent by her side without a single moment to bring him back to his morning nightmares. That's why he still doesn't tell her a thing.

After having picked up some auburn locs for her next weave, Marraine buys Kim a gold-plated pendant in the shape of Martinique. That evening, at the airport, he keeps it against his heart at the end of a chain on which Christian amulets have been collected since his birth.

Once on the plane, on the rocket to heaven on earth, Kim cries, his forehead against the window so that nobody will see him.

I did not know that.

Perhaps it's there, in that strange country, that Kim became a stranger, in that land where artificial paradises attract like honey flies children who hate their own bodies.

To Make Maman Proud

I CATCH UP WITH KIM in Nanterre, France. He is eighteen. He likes being in France. It's far away. It's an easy door to open on a faraway elsewhere. And it's not hard to get carried away: that's what you must do when you leave, you must love France. Love their cold their sky their food their museums their music and their thin-legged women. Kim likes France: France is beautiful.

But my oh my, is it cold. And the alcoholic remedies of his Northern friends aren't persuasive against this cold business.

"How do people who emigrate to Canada even do?" he asks Sébastien during the traditional bar crawl at the beginning of the school year.

"Maybe it's the people's warmth? I hear Quebecois are cool."

"Or maybe they drink even more than the French!"

Despite his attempts at debauchery with Sébastien before his departure, Kim has never seen as much alcohol as in Nanterre. A rather normal evening felled more bottle cadavers and drunken people in front of him than during his entire childhood. Before the so-called Celibacy Party, that strange nocturne full of precarious dances and stray laughter, he had never seen people vomit their alcohol in the gutter while laughing. "People say that Martinicans drink, but that's bullshit," he tells me on the phone the next day, stunned. "The French are the ones who drink! They're the ones who don't know how to drink!"

It's my third year at the Schœlcher Campus, in Martinique. I stayed on my foremothers' land, by conviction, and because I want to continue my initiation, the one Kim knows nothing about, but that I have the duty to complete, on this side of the ocean. I would never have sent Kim to France if I were his mother, but I am not his mother. So when he calls me, when he zig-zig-zag-zags on the phone between furor and fascination, I try to hush my own revolt to reassure him, to find the tender words to encourage him to meet share doubt open up give in all the while rolling my eyes on the other side of the line. I don't see anger break under his silences. And I bury in my mind, among other deadly ellipses, the words that could extend to my brother the helping hand he longs for. I should have told him what I thought then, I would have told him: "They know us better than us. They tell us stories about who we should be. They say be yellow and we turn to straw. They say you're drunk and soon, you're tipsy-gray. The sky is yellow through the sand at home, but it's blue because they decreed it so. The sea stinks of curdled blood at home, but it's crystal clear because they said so. And the blood of the Tropics is purulent, but it's warm and sweet in the throat of the other who knows everything. And you, my dear brother, pay no mind to their eyes that stare at you in the dark. Pay them no mind as long as you know who you are."

But like everyone, I killed my anger in my throat to protect him from it. Yet it is in our silences that lost children plant the seeds of their hatred.

Paris is beautiful, after all. Kim loves, in Paris. Friends for life, memories of soirées spent laughing to tears, funny tunes that don't move his heart, and an eternal party to forget the cold the smells the racism the police the struggle, the anthropology class where the only human gifted with reason seems to have a color different from his. He could stay. He shares a flat, a *toufe yenyen*-shoebox in Denfert-Rochereau, a one-bedroom the size of a studio. It's impossibly small, but it's Paris, and Goddamn it . . . when it's not raining, when it's not too cold, when you can take your time, when you're silly in love, Paris . . .

Kim seeks tenderness like a junkie rummages for crack on the ground in the streets of Foyal. He catches it in the middle of the void, he emerges from the water and he breathes. But the crystal rocks become rarer and rarer as the sun goes down. So you must face the incompressible waters of a humanity lost in the labyrinth of its own wealth. For even in the claustrophobic corners of a metro car, surrounded by hypnotized faces, lovers find in Paris a world where they can disappear and come together. Kim often lingers there on a seat, forgetting his station to drink them from afar, those couples on the lam who pluck each other's sighs, each other's gaze on the way. The hand weaves between pressed passengers to smooth a stray hair behind her friend's ear, and their smiles taut between their eyes devour one another. They aren't hungry for sex bodies fluids nor flesh. They drink in this moment the most precious beverage, all this amid the impossible din of line 5. She slips a message of no importance into the hollow of the pink ear. She grazes it with her lips. Her friend shivers, she responds, and they laugh together. They're in love. It was worth the trip, lovers canoodling on a bench, just as old Brassens sang it, who make you feel ashamed to disturb them. But they don't give a shit about the world, those people who love in Paris. It's their insolence that fascinates Kim. He worships their strength, he soaks it in as he follows in silence, from train to train, from time to time, people who love each other, to seize this love, understand it, and perhaps feel it land on his skin, adrift.

But Kim doesn't dare. Kim thinks beauty is for others, for those who were born here, for those whose freedom isn't a matter of debate. For him, beauty is a weapon to say what's good and to kill what's bad. To say what's just and to denounce the rest of the universe. For him, beauty is a scam dressed in Dior and perfumed with Chanel n° 5 to conceal the smell of the cadavers rotting under its frills.

Paris is not the Champs Élysées. Kim understood this pretty quickly because he never has the time to go there. Too expensive, that street made of glass is a permanent frustration for those who struggle to exist in the world's VIP section. Paris doesn't smell like perfume, in truth. Paris smells like piss on the sidewalk. White men treat it like their toilet, naked, shameless and fearless, imperial or cheeky, asserting their presence without any awareness of their omnipotence. Others slip by. Others must elbow their way in. Paris doesn't smell of warm bread and strawberries. Paris's smell is a cloying mix of fried Asian foods, Indian spices, and roasted lamb, in the side streets, the ones where people really live and where the world invited itself after having reclaimed its freedom. And in this ersatz of empire, White people walk briskly. And sometimes, they stop to stare at us.

Kim lacks the words to understand their empty eyes, their clenched jaws, their backs hunched over glass or paper screens, in silence, shut out from a love that bubbles beneath the surface and that no one can see anymore. In Paname's nagging tunes, Kim is at a loss for words, at a loss to understand the murderous fear of those among the French who are chained to a root, an origin.[7] Monsters always lie in wait, those who decide who must live and who must die, those who decide who is deserving of the life of human beings and who is deserving of the life of fish. They lie in wait, and their venomous voices spill into people's blood, even the blood of people in love.

One morning on the metro on his way to work, eyes low,

headphones on, Kim finds in his peripheral vision a Nazi tattoo circled with Wotansvolk triangles. He had just read a terrifying article about it on social media. The tattooed man ensnares Kim with his gaze, a gaze as blue as the ocean, framed by a sunny mane of hair, in the middle of a sandy white face. This island-made-man caresses his adornment with desire. In the midst of this crowd that ignores the danger, insignificant or worse, indifferent, Kim's heart beats the drums at the edge of a precipice.

Kim doesn't heal from this, from the cold in the flesh of the people. The frost on his skin, it's not the weather. It's the breath of ghosts who roam in the metro without quite knowing whether they lost love or if, in fact, they found a place to forget it existed. If only, if only those lost children could speak to one another.

Kim wraps himself in sun to cross the Parisian night. In his ears, the playlist of Maman's parties and his favorite album: Eugène Mona's. But when he is out of battery and silence burrows in his mind, Kim slips toward lands where the clamor of vengeance is the only thing that glows. He grabs hold of Léonide's words, words so often repeated that he knows them as well as the poems he recited at school. The ancestors are absent; they fear the ocean too much. But their words precede them and accidentally remain caught in the miraculous curls of my brother's hair. Those words from another world lull him, and he dreams with them.

In Régale, everyone is proud to know that Kim is in Paris. But Kim says nothing of his madness. He doesn't say that he stopped going to school in December and that he works at a fast-food joint, waiting for summer. No one would understand. No one would understand either why he rents an apartment for 1,000 euros per month in Paris proper even though an aunt by marriage extends him a sofa bed in her living room. He prefers silence and its torpor. At least, silence won't disappoint him. And in this silence, Kim spends beautiful hours in Paris.

"I could have stayed," he confides a few months later, before returning to the native land. "I could have loved that life, I could have dug my hole, I could finally have been myself in a place where I am no one, I could have forgotten the cold, the metro and even forgotten that my skin is black in a country stuffed with racists. I could have. When I think about it, when I see her face, her lips saying my name, her eyes that pierced right through me, I, too, could have stayed a little longer."

Kim loved someone in Paris, but he left them before I even knew their name. So Kim calls me, sobbing, alone in his empty flat, like a conch without a shell, an old spineless thing lost in a deadly place, without armor. Without pretext. And without a roof, because 1,000 euros per month is no life.

Kim throws out everything before taking the plane back. Some people love to keep trinkets and keepsakes from their college years. Photos, boho baubles that give Parisian chic. Kim has nothing of the sort. From his one and only trip, to London, he brought back nothing but a magnet shaped like a red phone booth. And he finds this uber-kitsch magnet so dumb, alone in his bag, that he leaves it in the garbage, too.

Kim's return is like a disappointment for our family. The ladies in Régale thought he'd become a day trader and then get engaged to a clean guy from the neighborhood. No one recognizes him when he comes back. The neighbors say that Kim has become hysterical. Me, I am so proud of my brother. In front of Marraine, who nearly faints when she hears her goddaughter referred to in the masculine, Maman chucks it all to a broken heart and fans her girlfriend while tolerating her string of supplications to the Most High. In the days that follow, Marraine and the neighborhood harass Kim with their intrusive questions. But Kim doesn't want to talk. What for? Who does he need to convince? Maman already knows. When Kim walked out through the airport's glass doors, when Maman opened her arms to him. When she told him I love you, like one reminds a child of a forgotten lullaby. Kim knew she knew. She had always known that Kim was a boy.

Kim moves in with Maman after that. Once again, he is a kid in her kingdom. He serves everyone during the parties, but he gets spoiled, too. He respects politeness and propriety and even appears with Maman at mass in Vauclin.

He accompanies her to all the baptisms. He even goes to all the funerals, then he organizes Maman's, conscientiously.

Cancer is a motherfucker.

To Burn the Trash

KIM TIDIES MAMAN'S HOUSE. I only take care of the garden. I empty the shed, I remove cumbersome objects, I plow the entire terrain to uproot our toxic plants, but I refuse to cross the threshold of this cursed house one more time. So Kim puts away Maman's life. Her keepsakes her treasures her baubles. He files her victories, her cries and her shames and he throws in the trash those useless things she left on her shelves and whose significance is unknown to him. The doilies, the recordings on audiocassettes, the unfinished crosswords, the travel keepsakes, and the faded shoes. Kim rented a dumpster, and he chucks everything in it.

Perhaps that's what we should have kept.

And everywhere, even after bleaching everything, Kim smells Maman's perfume. Her perfume, her perfume . . . it makes the walls smell of jasmine. Heady. Maman's perfume strips down the smell of lies in the whole house. The smell of bleach on the tiles, of fruit that fell from trees but was never picked up, the smell of the clothes of the dead who died but never left. The tin roof that leaks, the bidets, the car-tire swing that hangs from the mango tree like a cadaver, the ceiling that warps, and the floor.

Her perfume wipes away centuries of pain buried deep in the

humus. It is an elixir made of the tenderness of her eyes dressed in colors, the wisdom of her slightly oblique smile, the warmth of her breasts beaded with sweat, and her words, supple and intriguing, Maman's words, so mad with love that no one would have dared hang them at the gallows of incest. Maman's perfume doesn't know about Laurent's crimes. So its caress, for a little while longer, calms Kim's heart and delays his madness.

Two years after Maman's death, I send a tree pruner to trim the big trees that threaten the roof of the family home, once and for all, so I don't have to take care of it. Because I still refuse to go up to Régale, Kim goes there to keep an eye on the job. Nature seems poised to swallow the patio. He moves through the invasive lianas while distractedly glancing over at the woodcutters' cautious work. When the grand trees relent, the valley looks so much bigger from the guardrail. Kim stops wringing his hands and dreamily dives into it, lulled by the contemplative faraway voices of the past. Amid the vegetation, toward the city's center, a new neighborhood had sprouted since his childhood. Those are more recent homes, drawn like Maman's. At the bottom of this valley, Kim then recognizes the brand-new roof of his father's house, Laurent . . . And the chainsaw plays a sweet lullaby in his buzzing *kabech*-head. Already, in his mouth with clenched jaws, the troubling taste of blood arises. He no longer smells Maman's perfume.

To Reveal the Trickery

IN DILLON, CHIEF of Police Jean-Severine quickly identifies the cadaver of the first victim. Frédéric Justille, thirty-eight, head of his department at the tax office. It wasn't hard: his whole life was in his wallet. He died in the home of his mistress. A handful of neighbors said so.

On him, eighty euros in cash, two credit cards, and a brand-new smartphone. The murderer didn't even try to cover it up as a burglary. It would have been so easy. So many robberies go awry.

"The murderer wasn't a man," curtly retorts a neighbor hanging from his window. "It was a woman."

The chief of police hears a thousand more details from this voice falling from above. With a nod, she sends her second-in-command to talk to the man. The chief of police takes a deep breath, closes her eyes briefly and prays, in a secular silence, before turning to the second victim.

"Édith has been renting this house since she graduated from college, I think."

The pencil of Chief of Police Jean-Severine squeaks unpleasantly on the recycled paper of her notepad. She wonders if she has a pen in her bag. The neighbor continues.

"Yes, that's right. She had just finished her accounting degree when she moved to the neighborhood. My wife is the one who told me all about it. You should ask her instead."

"You're here right now, sir."

"Ok . . . so she was a beautiful young woman, ya know, strong, straight. She kept her hair natural, braided in crowns atop her head, ya know, it was very fashionable then. She still does it, I think. She is *happy, nappy* or something like that.[8] She was looking for a house for her and her boyfriend, Frédéric, the one who's lying on the floor there. My daughter said that Édith told everyone that Frédéric saw her at a party, danced with her, took her phone number and courted her for three months before shyly inviting her to a restaurant, and from there, things got heated, *an tjè koko*, a real love story. That was the sanctioned version. Respectable, ha!"

"And the real version?"

"The truth, little lady, is that they most likely *koké*-fucked on the first night because the child they had nine months later wasn't the fruit of the Immaculate Conception!"

"So Mr. Justille had been living here for six years?"

"No, no! He didn't live here! He is married!"

"Oh?"

"And for years, he and his wife had been trying to conceive! The poor lady would go to the Saint-Jean clinic. My cousin told me. She is a midwife there. But he, on the other hand, he got his treatment from Chango, and even more religiously, if you see what I mean . . ."

"Hum . . ."

"*Men ni sent-lan, ni Chango pa té pé ba yo an timanmay! Tjen-bwa* is the devil's work. Just a bunch of charlatans! My wife said that he cried so much in his mistress's lap that his tears penetrated her belly, and she got pregnant! Cute, no?"

"So Édith killed . . ."

"*Tjip, fè travay-zot*, I never said that. If Édith had wanted to kill Frédéric, she would have done so a long time ago, and she would have been cleaner, too. He was always at her house on Wednesday when his wife was taking her aqua bike class."

"You seem well-informed, sir . . ."

"It's my cousin. She works out with Mrs. Justille."

"The midwife?"

"No, a different one. Focus. You're making me lose my train of thought. It's not Édith! What was I saying?"

"He'd come on Wednesdays during her pregnancy."

"That's right. The guy promised her everything, ya know? House marriage trips clothes. He was loud, that's why the whole neighborhood could hear. It was on purpose. He was trying to just convince everyone! Pfff. And Édith listened. Divorce, big house in Terreville, a little trip to the Grenadines Isles, not a cruise, no! A private catamaran with a skipper! You can buy everything with the 40 percent bonus civil servants get for working here, right? And Édith listened. She's real calm, ya know? Always calm . . . and one day, *bidim*-pow! She yelled at him, her sister Kim was there too, I think. She yelled I tell you and I remember perfectly what she said, yes, perfectly, *woy! Mi kalté pawol!*"

"What did she say?"

"She said everything! She said: 'Don't touch me! I can't stand your weak touch and your breathing on my neck. When you touch me, I disappear. Why do you make people disappear?'"

"Ok, but . . ."

"She said: 'Leave, you useless fuck! Go lay your *wayayay* sperm in the belly of another *Négresse*! That's all you know how to do.' She said that exactly like I told you, ma'am, and after, the earth stopped shaking."

"And he left?"

"Yes. That was a month ago, I think. But he still comes from time to time. He babysits the little one here, two days a week, like that, and she, Édith, goes to rest at her house in Vauclin with her new guy. The marabout."

"And that new guy, could he be the killer?"

The neighbor stares into the void, shuts his eyes on an image that throws him into disarray, blinks them open, then looks straight at the detective. He says: "Ma'am, I told you, a woman did this."

To Offend the Church Roaches

THE *RAVETS LÉGLIZ*, those church roaches, look for me in Vauclin. People tell them: "*Fanm marabou-a? Yo ni an gro kay an fondok savann-lan ki ka mennen'w Makabou. Yo ni jaden, yo ni prin, yo ni sitron, yo ni razié ba tout maladi, yo sé pé ouvè an fawmasi!*"[9]

They know where to find my house and that magic is practiced there. Within fifteen minutes, they'll reach my neighborhood. Fifteen more to drive cautiously down the gravel road. And then, the team of budding, adventure-starved exorcists will need a solid half an hour to pray, encircle the place and prepare its ingress into my diabolical home.

Meanwhile, Ayo crosses the border into the world of the living. The air is denser on this side. She feels the bite of the sun's rays. She reacquaints herself with her gaunt body. Her bones are still marked by the blows that were intended to break her during her torture, and her heel is still sliced from the day she was caught marooning in 1820. Her eyes are blinded as she takes flesh on earth. She squints as she moves closer to her heiress's door.

Now that I see my house in a dream, I must admit the neighbors were right. With its walls painted with warm colors, it looks like a parody of the Quai Branly, that immense ethnographic museum in Paris. On the stoop, an enormous wicker basket overflows with African cloths and feathers. Past the front door, a room filled with drums from the four corners of the world, most of them out of tune. In the galley kitchen, the walls are covered with vaudou dolls lined up butt to butt, and Orisha figurines hang upside down from the ceiling. The workbench is blanketed with a forest of potted herbs, mostly imported, watered with a drip irrigation system. In the living room, leather armchairs abut Rastafari fabrics, even though Rastas are vegetarian. Absolute nonsense. Any vaudou novice, any adorer of Yemaya, any Chango disciple would consider this display of ignorance and cheap junk with utter contempt. Despite always feigning expertise, the adepts of the marabout have never understood a thing about the eclectic maze that is my house. Yet my walls hold a precise meaning, for the wise one who can find it and ignore the things of no importance.

Ayo's incarnated ghost enters my home as she would her own bathroom. In the first room, she picks the only tuned drum from all the others. It comes from her country. Bought for a pretty penny from slave traders on the black market, we've kept it for two centuries and it's still here. It's an okonkolo, a bata drum. With it, we establish the link between the two worlds. She touches it: she can touch it. She beats it. It resonates. She plays it. It wakes me from my slumber.

I hate being awakened by surprise. Morning alarms never bear good news. While she waits for me to get out of bed, Ayo glides toward the living room, guided by a copper line I threaded for her through the kitchen. She plucks a golden nesting doll from the ceiling and gleans a handful of cowry shells from its bosom.

When I push my bedroom door open, I see the pearly currency arranged on the coffee table in a water fountain. I understand that one of Oshun's daughters wants to consult with me. It's been a solid ten years since I've been summoned. So I sit down on the goat skin spread on the floor in front of the fountain, I raise my eyes to the gaunt and evanescent body of my illustrious foremother. And my heart beats fast.

To Bring Our Story to a Close

"I LIKE THE kid, you know."

In the *kaz*, Kim shaves Laurent with his knife and cheap shaving cream. He wipes the salt-and-pepper bristles on a warm towel and continues, very softly. "My nephew. Cédric. My sister took him everywhere, he never missed an Ash Wednesday mass, and he was at all the soirées the carnival runs the *beach parties*.[10] The child was my sister's war trophy. She put him on display for the world to see. She put him on display to proclaim her hard-earned freedom. She didn't owe anything to anyone anymore. Not anyone. Not even my mother.

"Cédric is a perfect little choir boy cast in a mold made of holy water and good behavioration. *Ti boug-la ni an bon lédikasion . . .* Men in this country, they are at their best at that young age, when they are too small to hurt anyone. He learned to read this year, so he reads stories to Édith in the afternoon so that she can close her eyes smiling. *An bon timanmay, dous kon siwo batri,* sweet, sweet like sugarcane syrup. You see, he must stay that way, he must stay innocent, so that he can't hurt anyone, so he can't become like his father. Édith is doing everything she can to prevent it, you know?

She advocates against domestic violence, she reads books in English about raising Black boys. Sometimes, she talks to me about them, but I don't understand a thing to that bullshit, even though *I*'m a Black boy! She tries, you know? She does everything she can to give herself the illusion that she is winning. But little Cédric is the blood of his *initil*-useless father. He is the blood of his bastard grandfather, you see, Laurent? And you're not even the only motherfucker who spoiled the child's genes. Cédric is also the blood of the White man who screwed Marie-Magdeleine in a sugarcane field, took her child away from her to teach her God knows what in his Creole home, whatever it was that those people did back then with our bodies our arms our sexes our flesh, which adorned their glossy parquet like furniture, our ebony wood, which shined their locust cabinets. My nephew is the blood of those people who sowed violence in Léonide's body before sending her back to her mother at the sight of her first period, too Black to be White in Didier, too White to be Black in Régale. And loveless. Loveless."

The knife nicks Laurent. But the blood doesn't pearl. Kim continues.

"I loved him, little Cédric. But he had to die. I could no longer stand his face his eyes his gaze. I could no longer stand to recognize your features in such a sweet being. I don't even know how Édith could stand it, and you know what? She couldn't. She beat him every day. I saw her. I'm not lying. And it's you she was beating through him, you bastard. But it wasn't revenge, no. It was your own arms she opened, too. The violence you put in my sister's body when you raped her, she never healed from it and she passed it on to her son. He was going to end up like you, he was also going to live to hurt. I am sure of it. It was already too late. I saw him with his paper heroes, virile and macho, I saw him with his dolls. There was no doubt. The poison had already reached his heart. If the child had lived, it would have been yet another generation degenerated by violence. I did what had to be done. I brought our story to a close. Édith will be furious, of course, but she'll understand, in time. The child had to die. I had to kill him. With any luck, next time, Édith will have a daughter steeped in her power. And she won't have anything to fear, thanks to me."

Foyal

"I still had the freedom to choose the time and place of my rage. When my throat would bow in a torment of blood, I would swallow my anguish and it would slither down to my stomach like a snake. I knew how to digest it in the acid of my entrails. And I would tell my rage: now is not the time. You say I wasn't ready, you say you were my arm raised as a shield against the storm but no. No, you didn't avenge me, no. You merely stole from me the last of my freedoms."

TRANSCRIPT OF ÉDITH'S JUDICIAL TESTIMONY AGAINST KIM

To Put an End to the Indivision

KIM LEFT MAMAN'S HOME three years ago. Since then, the house has been gathering dust. Never rented nor sold, all because of this matter of indivision, which Kim never tried to understand. I'm the one who's been taking care of it. I used to listen to his godmother and Maman cackle for hours about family matters. I am better suited than Kim to pretend to court people we don't know in front of rich notaries we don't know either. Just one appointment was enough to nauseate Kim and make him give up. The notary said:

"It's so common in our little territories that the will brings together two families that knew each other . . . without really knowing each other! Imagine that! Your grandmother Sidonie is the sister of the mother of Laurent Josephin, your father!"

"No," I retorted. "That woman is not part of the family. My grandfather raised her out of wedlock, and everyone knows she is not his."

"Ma'am . . . the paperwork is all in order. Consequently, as we wait for further developments in this matter, considering that your great-grandmother Léonide's house was never officially bequeathed to you, it belongs to you just as much as it belongs to your father Laurent, and his potential brothers and sisters."

Kim got up and exited the room. He never set foot in the notary's office again.

Shortly after, Kim took a flat in the city, and that's where he's been ever since. It's impossibly small. It has no history. He no longer has a garden. But at least, at night, his sheets and his paperwork no longer hang around the smell of crime.

The city is noisy. It's full of cockroaches. Kim has never been afraid of cockroaches. But since he's been in the city, he wants to turn into a bird of prey every time he sees one. Cockroaches are harmless, unless you become their prey. Kim grew up in the countryside, he's seen his fair share of critters strolling along the walls since childhood. But before the city, he had never seen an army of cockroaches colonize a dumpster. An army.

Sometimes, when in the middle of the night, Kim hears them rapping at the pipes, when he sees their shadow slice through the glow of the streetlight, at night, when he can almost hear them talking fucking breathing, at night Kim tells himself that in Foyal, we humans live as clandestine migrants in a civilization of cockroaches. One night, when he had stayed up to twist his dreadlocks and was dozing off in his tiny bedroom, he imagined a kingdom of cockroaches where the cockroach queen had taken it upon herself to enslave all the other insects. And while the cockroaches paraded in the streets of *lanvil*-downtown, the other insects slaved away in the trash. And the swarmage of the city was their empire. Kim dreamed all of it up one night. Kim dreamed up the empire of the cockroaches that had conquered Martinique, and it was just like the world but without humans and their treasons. It was a world where all that was left of humans was their bones, bleached down to the marrow by the hairy legs of giant armored cockroaches. But this land had been cursed without them, before them, it had always been cursed, it had always been a land of suffering where the whip cracks so that we can rise and bow down every morning that the good cockroach God makes.

Each day that comes. It starts all over again. This island just doesn't know when to quit. This city of cockroaches is a sick heart, but it's a heart for the taking. Kim is smitten by this woman-city. He lost his mind for her. He left the *morne* for her. It wasn't for the love of cockroaches nor for the love of noise and dust. Kim never was a city rat. But now he wanted to possess the city, he wanted to walk in the streets of Fort-de-France one day and say: "This is Fort-de-my-home."

A vain and far-fetched dream. One day, he told me on the phone:

"If the kingdom of the cockroaches loses the garbage war, Foyal will be the new Disneyland."

"You and your cockroaches . . . you're nuts."

"I don't mind negotiating with cockroaches. There are more bothersome invaders. See, the pale skins have invaded *lanvil* since New Year's Day. They visit the *Nègres*, they go into their *kaz* to see how they live, they trace paths of conquest with their ratty old shoes."

"The tourists come with their cash, Kim."

"And their red faces, speckled with tumors, so proud to be in the isles, like Gramps in the good old days of the colony, yeah! I see them every day on the *malecon*, they walk by the statue of Belain d'Esnambuc, that motherfucking colonizer, and they take selfies with him. And then they walk up Rue Blenac, they lift their sunburnt noses toward our wrought iron balconies and they say, *It's nothing like the metropole*, they say, *with a fresh coat of paint it would look just like Bahia*, they say, *doesn't it look just like Latin America?*"

"Isn't that a compliment?"

"Édith, in their mouth it means that it's almost poor almost backward almost quaint, and when you go beyond the cobblestones, it's almost like a museum dedicated to the time when Paris was so much more beautiful than the colonies, when Paris was so much more ahead of us, and it reassures him, the prole-on-his-discount-vacation who drags his old suburban sandals on the pier. It reassures him to be White amid the misery of the world, to be French in the Caribbean. It reassures him to strut, belly hanging out, down the shiny pavement of conquered lands and to say here the pavement shines because I willed it so. I'm telling you, Édith, their world only makes sense as long as a couple of pale skins can walk across La Savane Park, snap photos of the great White names on the front of the Schœlcher Library and judge, displeased, the decapitated statue of the empress!"[11]

I let Kim soar on his historical flights of fancy. He went to college, he knows what he is talking about, apparently. But he doesn't hold the key to his own world. He still feels for it, over and over, in the dark. His thirst for knowledge gets lost in the labyrinth of his anger, but it has been proclaimed, it is there. It's certainly like this that one day, forsaken at the impasse of our commonly cultivated silences, we lost him.

I interrogate the Breaths, and they take me there, to the day where everything fell apart, in a detail, a single, insignificant detail brimming with violence.

A sand mist suffocates Fort-de-France's sky like a storm that won't rain. Overwhelmed by the heat in his one-bedroom apartment, Kim takes refuge in the supermarket by the shore: it is air-conditioned. Kim fills up his cart. He takes his time. He dissects the labels while chewing over his rancor. At checkout, he pays too much. Outside, the sun seems to be diffracted in each grain of sand. He squints as he shuffles down the crosswalk and sets his shopping bag down in front of a travel agency to catch his breath. On the window, he reads: "Trip to Indochina, the Enlightenment tour."

Indochina.

The Enlightenment.

That day, for the first time, Kim wants to kill someone.

He should have left that day. He should have left town while he still could. When the swell skimmed the ashes of the cruise ships, when the backward wind brought back the dull sounds of drunken tourists, when the port released shit and garbage from the whole world in its waters and when ads for Jeeps replaced graffiti on the walls. When a mural of Eugène Mona's face on Rue République renamed Rue Indépendance was covered by a billboard for the next national elections.

In the days that follow, Kim feeds his revolution. He re-reads the books he wasn't given as a child, thrifted in Paris. The history of the Viet Cong the Fellagha the Kikuyu the Kalinagos. Drunken on musty paper, he immerses himself in the web and latches onto the peremptory voices of modern-day priestesses who, like me, wear their hair in crowns. He discovers himself in those faces that look like his, in those words that speak his rage, in those histories he craves, in that war he longs for. The young priestesses of the web sell love for cheap, glorifying for a flat fee the exploits of the goddesses and queens of the past, forgetting that we, the Black women of this country, are neither tyrants nor aristocrats nor immortals, but what difference do details make, as long as we are given the crown we had been coveting elsewhere? What difference does it make, he tells me, when I confront him with the details? Why dwell on the details? Hadn't the essential always been concealed from him? Kim picks what's essential to him now. Kim sinks his entire self into the flux of words that say what he wants to hear. He is once again in the eye of the hurricane, waiting for the day of the great reckoning. The voice of Léonide, in harmony, sings for him the praises of tomorrow. So Kim arises as a hero. He arises armed. He arises clothed in the fantasy of a Kemetic warrior, vengeance's foot soldier.

To Blow Everything Up

ON A FAT TUESDAY MORNING, Kim skips his turn.

The hour is still blue and the scattered city already buckles under the weight of a swarm of insolent drums. It vibrates, completely, ready to take flight or crumble to pieces. Carried by the rising swell of snare drums, the crowd tumbles down the boulevard, hopping feet together toward the sky. And the defiant chants of incubuses dressed in pajamas for the carnival swear to always fight against oppression by kicking dead horses and reciting cynical incantations.

"*Bann Makoumè!*" Kim yells in his bath, even though he has sworn never to soil his mouth with that word again. But the crowd's wings rush deep into *lanvil*'s guts, climb up the water main, and squirt between the tiles of Kim's bathroom walls. The *Nègre* tidal wave wins and drowns him. Kim dives into the soapy water. He can breathe now.

He should have left, before the mirth invaded the decrepit streets and painted the dirty walls with feathers and sparkles. "I should have left," Kim tells himself, over and over. He should have left before the trafficked motors of that army of *bradjak*-junkers started its morning serenade, which sounded so much like a battery of machine guns even though it never hurt anyone other than the ears of the children of *lanvil.* He should have left to go wade in the serene waters of the northern rivers, where the souls of the real maroons are laid to rest, instead of playing hide and seek in the streets of *lanvil* with *Nèg gwo siwo.*[12] He should have run far away from the carnival and its mirages to seek, in the red soil, the Breaths' true war cry.

But Kim stayed.

Nearly dead, he emerges from below and swallows air to survive. The drum beats, incessantly, everywhere, on the walls, the mirror, inside his waterlogged flesh, on his feverish brow and he can no longer discern what is up inside outside. Kim cannot escape that drum that beats the *Nègre*'s call. He can no longer avoid it. The drum takes everything, it even steals Kim's thoughts. It takes up residence in his mind. His heart beats fast. Kim gets up and mumbles senselessly, without knowing what he wants what he is. He is sober yet already drunk on music, dizzy with vibrations as one is after love. The drum, a large plastic barrel beaten with a mallet, marches below his balcony and rings in Vaval's honor. Vaval, the idol of carnival: five vertical meters of irreverence and papier-mâché perched upon a float. This year, to incarnate Vaval, the artists sculpted him, in secret, into the body of a corrupt politician. Ass out, the effigy's anus brims over with bank notes, and its golden teeth crunch into chlordeconed yams. It's been two days, two full days already since Vaval began parading the streets with his court, one hundred thousand strong, walking in step and spewing inanities. The drums beat to suck the latecomers in. Kim resists. The drums demand that the island's blood be spilled in the streets to elevate Vaval to the pinnacle of his glory. Kim balks.

Kim almost feels seasick. He gets out of the water and pats his skin already beaded with sweat. In front of his mirror, Kim looks at herself naked, as if her body suddenly made sense to her . . . Who cast this spell on her? She doesn't want to partake, no, she doesn't want to run the carnival, she doesn't want to reverse the roles, to upset her world, she doesn't want to return to this body from which she had ripped herself out. "Enough!" she screams at the demons who try to suck her into the crowd. Fear and nausea force her away from her reflection. But the drum is stronger than her will. Kim's neck relaxes, her hands petal open, her hips tremble. "Am I cold?" she wonders. No, she is dancing.

Walk a little bit to warm yourself up, Kim. Dawn kills. You must bring into motion the warm blood that burns us.

At the foot of the building, the drum keeps beating. It spends on the pavement the sentimental sap of a crowd lost with love, sweating its grief and shouting in a contagious mass its joy to be freed from its sacred mission.

Kim slips on his boxer shorts and puts on his shirt angrily. He doesn't want to dance he doesn't want to pretend to be anot/her. He is angry with this world that beats the drum at dawn, angry with this masquerade, angry with this people that doesn't know where to place its presence. He asks the Breaths: "What's with this absurd need to take to the streets once a year? Where was this crowd when we needed to topple complicit governments? Where was this crowd when we needed to rip out the poison from the soil of our heroes? Where was this crowd when, with the survival of a people hanging in the balance, we needed to upend paper statutes? Where was it, this people, awake at the crack of dawn to run the carnival, when it needed to make a break for its freedom instead?"

Called by the tide of nationalist flags flowing under his balcony, Kim takes to the street. He is armed. He doesn't hate his own blood yet; he wants to believe, still, that on this Fat Tuesday, the blood of the *Nègres* will shed the blood of the snakes. He doesn't dress up. He doesn't play a part. He doesn't reverse his role. Or so he thinks.

Faded jeans, a red t-shirt, exhausted sneakers, and in his oversized pocket, his knife. When he goes down the stairs of his Foyal apartment, two months before killing my son, Kim is a foot soldier whose heart beats to the sound of the drum, but out of sync.

Never in a million eyes have we ever been so close to having a country of our own, when the boulevards, aglow with the day's first lights, fill with flags drawn by our hands. The green and the black mingle with red devils as if today would go down in history as the day of our independence. No more civil servants or terrified cowards in the streets, only Martinican men and women jubilantly celebrating their national day. With the *ravèt-légliz*-church-roaches cowering under their beds, what remains is the all-mighty power of Africa, shaken from its slumber, calling upon the bones of the dead, the burnt skin of men and women who lost their names in the clay many moons ago to spring from the earth. And the monsters of our world become the kings and queens of our glorious march.

The carnival groups walk through *lanvil* armed with a fanfare, flags tutus kawaii umbrellas lace-trimmed madras varnished banana-tree leaves and whips to shoo away bad spirits. And in this soup, by the thousands, carnivaling men and women live in cadence, and for three days, they sing everything that's forbidden and play all the games God has forbidden. The world is upside down, no more race, no more jobs, no more morals, no more church, no more lies, no more sermons or laws except those we wrote to reinvent the most elementary gestures. Totalitarian, the carnival's law imposes its march its god its road regulations its language its music its preachers its myth its history and its memory. Enraptured in the illusion of a final We, there is just one people, one people, undivided, that shouts in unison under the window of the French prefect: "*Yo pa lénou antré. Yo pa lé nou antré! Aux Antilles, yo ba nou dlo kontaminé au chlordécone. Obéissance à la loi? Ay kokémanman'w!*"[13] And the drum loses it, the snare machine-guns the sun, the crowd metamorphoses into an immense and strident throat! Stomping hard enough to blow the asphalt to bits, a menacing army of glitter comes hurtling: "My heart beats fast, I will destroy everything!"

And the blind think it's just a trendy song.

And the deaf think the carnival is a sexual farandole.

And the ignorant burrows his head in the sand so as not to see the land he conquered burn down.

And with good reason. The carnival tastes, smells, and sounds like a revolution, but nothing happens. Vaval's soldiers are armed with satin and dirty cotton rags. Vaval's soldiers walk on stilettos and shuffle, sex first. And on the *malecon*-pier, facing the sea, Vaval's soldiers insult everything and the sun, but don't dare touch a hair of the colonizer's statue that towers defiantly in their path. So Kim curses with the crowd, but it's the crowd he insults. He even insults the Breaths for their indifference. Kim curses, frowning, with his hand in his pocket, nervously gripping the handle of his knife. His eyes snake through the ranks of the useless army. His heart beats fast. He wants to blow everything up. He wants to smash the statues, set the prefecture ablaze, rip the flags, bring down the crucifixes, destroy, one stone at a time, each trace that history built upon the blood of his ancestors. He wants to burn down the damned city that raped Léonide. His heart beats . . .

Kim is ready to kill someone. But he doesn't know who yet.

On the first day of Lent, the silence buzzes.

Kim is sprawled out on his mattress on the floor. It's still dark out, and his black satin costume sticks to his thighs. They burned Vaval the night before, and the rum scorched his insides, carrying with it the energy of his audacity. "That's the only thing carnival is good for," moans Léonide at the edge of the world. "It drains the blood of the revolutionaries. It's not Vaval we burn on Ash Wednesday, it's our own power."

Léonide, the Hanged One, will not let her protégé's blood drain out in a tranquil Lent. The powerful witch draws deep from the well of her wrath and selects an insect as her emissary to wake him up. For the task, the queen of spells bewitches the smallest enemy of mankind and sends it on a commando mission.

Zig-zig-zag-zagging against the cold wall of Kim's bedroom, a mosquito. Zigging and zagging, its frail body searching for blood. A bold arc near his ear: It whirrs in Kim's welcoming lobe. The mosquito loves blood. This dawn, the mosquito wouldn't mind feasting on Kim's blood. But the mosquito net stands between its desire and its target.

Thwarted, the mosquito lets out a wail, sensual and nagging, strident to the ear of the slumberer. Transparent, straight, diligent, the mosquito net withstands every assault. So Léonide's soldier cannot pass through and it waits, patient, present. It whispers sweet words to Kim through the net while he sleeps. It harasses him when he wakes up and keeps him in the moist limbo of an unfinished dream. There, the mosquito slumbers with him when the sun shines bright. It waits for darkness to return before roaring again. It waits for a cloud to obstruct the red venetian blinds desiccated by the sun. And there, it surveys the net, searching for the largest pores, for a tear to penetrate. A wound. An open wound, in the net, from long ago, when a violent gesture opened a microscopic gash into the fabric of Kim's consciousness. Just a few millimeters. No one can see it. No one will see it. That's where the mosquito enters. In Kim's consciousness. It bites him. Kim awakens in the morning. He remembers his wound. He suffocates. And his heart beats fast.

To Stop the Noise

THE NOISE NEVER stops in the city. It lingers.

The noise is like a fragrant sap that never stops oozing. It starts to thicken the arteries of *lanvil*-downtown at dawn and begins to smoke when the day warms up. Sublimated, the noise then pulls old tunes escaped from radio sets toward the sky and it pierces through the sandy haze carried by the winds from the Sahara Desert. Saturated with our words our cries, the noise leaps up to the troposphere, hooks on a jetliner, and carries elsewhere the echo of the feeling that an island belongs to us. The noise, in the morning, would scream so loudly against the walls of Foyal that it would cover Kim's childhood cries. So Kim loved this noise, and he wouldn't have minded getting lost in it forever.

Kim decides to kill Frédéric just a few weeks before executing his plan.

It happens on a Wednesday, downtown. Kim returns from visiting Uncle Servan. He was Maman's godfather. The old man, whom he hadn't seen in ten years, doesn't have much time left, so Kim came to him as he was before his transition so as not to hasten his passage. Uncle Servan found his grand-goddaughter lovely, asked her about Paris, reminisced, with a damp eye, about an old flame he had met there after the Algerian War. Then, tired, Kim left him in the glow of this smiling memory.

His good deed done, Kim takes a taxico back to Foyal, to go home to Rue Lamartine. Pulling into the depot, he is always fascinated by the beauty of the bay. Only in the brouhaha of gossip, music, and insults that reign in these jam-packed vans does he find a moment to let his eyes escape further than his arms to see, straight in front of him, the blue of the sea evaporating into the sky. The air is pure that day, and the bay unfurls all the way to the mountains of Trois-Ilets. Boats loll on the sparkling waters, and people stroll, seemingly aimless, on the shore.

Kim leaves the taxico's disorder with a sigh, elbowed by a matronly woman in a hurry behind him. On the asphalt, the noise catches up to him, and he drags his feet. At Rue Isambert, he immediately recognizes Frédéric from afar, with his Panama hat purchased for too much money in a boutique in Trois-Ilets. Kim has seen Frédéric at my home almost every Wednesday since Cédric's birth. Although he never liked him much, he was always polite to my son's father. But it has been a while now since I gave Frédéric his notice. And if I don't talk to him, Kim doesn't talk to him either. So Kim has no desire to see Frédéric. He would cross the street if he could. But the roads of *lanvil*-downtown don't let dogs without leashes set their paws out of the gutter. Kim is caught in a potholed bottleneck between a row of cars and a wall covered with a Xan mural. Frédéric is caught, too.

Frédéric doesn't know Kim like that, he has never seen him saddled with the feminine garments associated with the sex assigned to him at birth. For Frédéric, the woman in front of him is nothing but a piece of flesh gift-wrapped in tissue paper decorated with pornographic drawings.

Usually, Kim lowers his eyes when this happens. The feminine garb makes him less reckless. So usually, he lowers his eyes. He shuts the windows and keeps walking. But that day, after the carnival, after the long sleepless nights spent listening to Léonide's mosquitoes from afar, Kim has no intention of bowing in front of this man he despises. He wants to see his face when he recognizes him. So Kim squares up to him, all weapons out. He knows exactly what he will tell him if he dares open his mouth to address him.

But Frédéric rips Kim's garments with his eyes. He licks his lips. He is a few paces away. With his hands in his pockets, he rubs something against his left thigh. The air around him seems dense, and he takes it in, swimming free stroke in his fishbowl. He is right at home when he gazes at Kim. He puckers his lips. Closer, and he begins to breathe loudly. Closer yet, he sucks the saliva on his tongue with a noise. He is right in front of Kim. He says: "*Vini sisé mwen.*"

It's original. Normally, it's Whore, Skettel, *Gwo-bonda*-fat-ass, *Ya sa la*, or just Psst. But Frédéric uttered a complete sentence. By the time Kim is done studying the linguistic complexity of his Kreyol intervention, the guy is long gone, and Kim said nothing, did nothing. Because of the shock. The literary quip disrupted the script he had sketched. Kim keeps walking, spewing a litany of idiotic deprecations to explain his *ababa*-stupid silence. He only emerges from his stupefaction when he reaches the red light at Charles-de-Gaulle Boulevard. He murmurs an incantation: "My body, my body, inhabit my spirit once more. I feel you somewhere close. My body, stay my body. Stay with me."

There is no air in the city.

We bake under tin roofs and the wind doesn't whoosh through the old cinder block shacks. No park, no stream to pluck out a soothing breath. They just carved up boulevards and threw some grass on a square, but Kim sees no benches there to plop down his carcass, deboned by the blow of those three words.

He walks for a while under the sun, without remembering where he is going. "*Vini sisé mwen*" echoes like an old zouk song in his *flègèdè*-deflated head, he doesn't even hear the two men by the prefecture building who glide their insanities on his skin and bite it without even touching it.

Kim never told me that story.

He never told it to anyone. He doesn't think I would find the words. He is not wrong. My feminism is cowardly. I shout loudly but I don't do much. It's my war strategy. I am not ashamed of it. If he had told me, I would have grumbled a bit, performatively, against those patriarchal soldiers who patrol our streets. I would have shooed away the topic of Frédéric with a sibylline *tjip*. And quickly, I would have told Kim to stop whining. Stop whining and keep going.

Then Frédéric raped a woman.

That's why Kim killed him.

At least, that's what he always told the cops.

He finds out about it on his way to watch my son Cédric in Dillon. Two women are chatting in front of the bakery near the market, where people sell coconut water in bottles. Kim is waiting for a market vendor to get a bag of guavas to make juice. It's Lent. The weather is beautiful. Women are hot in the faux-satin gowns they don to go pray at Saint Thomas Church. The church always puts on a show. Kim likes to wander around it on Saturday mornings as he steps off the bus. Then, he tells me all about it as I pack my bag for Macabou:

"The priest is this young guy from around here who received the Holy Spirit from Jesus himself. He is so wrapped in fabric, it looks like he could walk on water."

"Stop blaspheming in front of my son, Kim."

"Wait, wait, there's more! Listen to this. Apparently, he performs exorcisms, and he calls upon both saints and orishas during purification séances. Maman would have loved him."

"Did you see it with your own two eyes to talk all this nonsense? You seem well-informed."

"But no one has seen it for real! No one would admit it, but everyone talks about it in the neighborhood. Stop pretending, you know this better than I do, I'm sure!"

"Mmh . . ."

"Apparently, it's better than chemo. The guy is a real star. All the *ravèt-légliz*-church-roaches, men and women all the same, literally ejaculate, screaming Amen, as he blesses them."

"Kim!"

Eavesdropping on the two *makrels* waiting for their bottle of coconut water, Kim smiles and tells himself that his description is hardly exaggerated. These women are in the throes of such a postcoital delirium that they don't even hear themselves talk, they don't even see that everyone is listening to the inanities they shout to high heaven. And they say:

"*Boeing, yo ka krié'y Boeing. Misié-a ja ni konmen ich an péyi-a, é I bizwen mété an lot adan bouden kousin-mwen an.*"

"*Sé tifi-a osi pou séré janm-yo.*"

"*Y pa mandé'y lapèmision. Boug-la pa sa mandé lapèmision.*"[14]

"*Woy . . .*"

"May the Lord forgive him. And may the Lord also forgive that girl! Why would you let an old man like that come near you unless you're asking for trouble?"

"But they know it, no? They see. I'm not going to feel sorry for those girls, *gadé yo ka maché toutouni toupatou*, Jesus, Mary, Joseph. Naked I tell you. The devil doesn't have to try very hard to enter your body when you put no obstacle in front of him."

"*Ou ni rézon*, it's true it's true, but the girls aren't the devil. Thatan is the devil himself. Pray for them, Christ will save them. But let the devil take Boeing straight to hell! I tell you, *tjip*, that guy is a scourge."

Boeing, a rocket that crosses the sky. Boeing, like the turgid curve of those who carry within the tomorrows of unfortunate days. Boeing, a rocket that dances and runs on the hot sand. Boeing Boeing . . . just a funny little ditty we sprinkle on children to tell them about life, life here, where guys roll on their sweet tongues the dumplings of their excesses. Boeing went everywhere and everywhere he shone and danced in the sky before disappearing in a cloud. And his tomorrows blossomed in sighs on the mattresses of unloved forlorn women, women who quickly too quickly got over letting Boeing's white blood run down their black skin.

Boeing. It's an old Creole song that always floated in my home when I was pregnant. One of those fluttery mazurka tunes that tells and retells our memories, our history, the history of the people who are from here, and of the guys *san-fouté*-no-shame who are good for nothing but digging that history into people's bellies.

Frédéric liked it when I called him that. And I called him Boeing.

So Kim learned in the street that Frédéric roamed all over and that all over he picked up lapidated hearts. And sometimes, when he alighted, he reaped people, people who weren't ripe yet.

To Break the Circle

KIM'S APARTMENT HAS a balcony that overlooks *lanvil*-downtown, hardly bigger than a folding seat, but an ideal *makrelaj*-lurking vantage point from which to let his eyes dawdle over other people's lives while he waits for his own to pass him by. It's the kind of square balconies that hang over the street. People walking below have no idea that it is above them, drawing wrought iron arabesques against the sky. Kim has one of those small balconies on the third floor above Rue Lamartine. China is on the first floor, Cuba to the right, Syria on the same floor, but it's Venezuela that lives in his living room, with its commercial bachata music woven all throughout the day from a poorly tuned radio set. Kim learned Spanish while fulminating loudly against his melomaniac neighbors.

At night, Kim wedges his body on the balcony to smoke a joint or simply to enjoy some fresh air. Gaze at the sky. He can see the apartment across the way. Indians. He never sees them at home, their window is obstructed by a one-way mirror pane that reflects the lights of the Trenelle Citron neighborhood. From his balcony, Kim cannot hear the frogs. But sometimes, late in the night, he sees fireflies.

The church bells awaken Kim every morning in Foyal. He finds them very beautiful. Some people hate them. Sometimes, the neighbors curse their echoes in Spanish, especially on mornings that follow big celebrations . . . *Por Dios, ¡maten a ese maricon!* Kim finds it funny to hear bachata-loving Venezuelans blaspheme against a good church bell recital. Kim doesn't have a statue of the Virgin Mary in his living room. But he loves church bells. He loves feeling their vibrations in the air and in his blood. The bells grip you right there, in the flesh. First, they ring only to tell the time. Then, their rhythm picks up a bit. They let out loud, high-pitched notes, like they're biting something. Kim loves this moment, when they become unhinged, that's when they wake everybody up. Dissonance. Notes that just won't fall right irritate. But they lull Kim. Difference comforts him. And bang, the big bell is at it again, it swings its body from left to right, we stagger with it. Once, it made Kim seasick, as if he were in the hold of the boat that goes to Saint Lucia. And then the music drifts away, it surfs out on the morning's waves. Small bells shiver delicately, like in fairy tales. Kim sees himself again, as a child, in his bed, telling himself stories while . . .

And the day comes. And Kim is no longer the same. He can't open his eyes, he waits, one hour perhaps, for the last vibration sprawled in his belly to come out through his throat. He needs to scream, nothing comes out. He needs to scream. Nothing comes out.

Kim has already decided to kill his father. Kim has already decided to kill Frédéric. He can no longer stand to breathe the air of a world where crimes remain unpunished.

But according to the Breaths, it is much later, on his balcony, that Kim decides to commit one murder too many, the murder that stole everything from me, the murder that even took the love I had for my own brother.

Since his encounter with the Saint-Thomas devotees, Kim spins without being able to hold on to a single thought. He spins his wound, he smokes it, drinks it, twists it in his head, and it hurts. In his inner trance, he kills his father, he kills Laurent, then he sees his tomorrows all laid out in front of him, each one the same as the day before. He sees men rip out vulvas and shackle his lineage, over and over, in a well of silence and screams. And on this thread, the drug's smoke rings make him bend sideways and he sees, he sees that there never was a lineage. He sees that history is not a straight line but a loop, made of perpetual returns to chains, rapes, and torments, at the center of which he stumbles, nauseous. It has to stop. He doesn't know how to stop it.

Kim spends Lent on an empty stomach and vomits every time he tries to eat. He is dizzy. He walks in a circle, and draws circles in chalk, on the floor, on the walls, without knowing why, tracing in his trance doors for the spirits who for centuries have been demanding vengeance in the absence of justice. And then, one night, Kim loses it and breaks the circle with a raging kick when he hears, under his balcony, the poetess of *lanvil*-downtown announcing the apocalypse once more.

"Come out come out come out! The God. The God has been announced! He wears the judge's wooden clogs. Bitter, those who know the place of the dead and the time of the living. The God is coming. He knows the blood you have spilled! Satan! Come out come out come out! Your body is weary under the talons of the saints! Here! The hour of your judgment has come! Yes! Obatala! Adonai! Take the cold sweat glued in long cracked streaks along my temples. Demon! Time is calling you to other lands where no one will ever sin again. Come out come out come out in the life after death, after death . . . after the glorious time of the false people.

"Come out come out come out of my wounded body and give the golden sun's bleeding heart to what's left of time."

Kim is hot. There is no more room in his body, in his skin. He must get out. He gets out. On this feverish night in Foyal, Kim gets up from his faux-leather armchair, crosses his living room in three paces, slips into a t-shirt he finds on the floor, opens the door and then slams it shut on all the lies. And Kim walks. He is not afraid of anything, he is like a *chien fer* set loose in La Savane Park, the wind caresses his smooth skin, black and silvery under the full moon, his gait is light, agile, frank. There, amid the lonesome beauty of this garden, Kim is the master of *lanvil*. That night in Foyal, Kim walks. He takes the boulevard to Rue Arago, then he rounds the corner at Rue Perrinon and walks, straight ahead. First, he looks at the asphalt, black and shiny under a fine layer of miraculous dew on a day without rain. The noise everywhere hushes in his eyes. Around him, he no longer sees the deafening purr of the air conditioning units whose stench still hugs the shoreline at midnight. He glides alone under the wind's gaze, and he stares at his feet, free from shackles. To walk. He thinks about his father. He thinks about himself. He thinks about the body of his sister, crushed, the body of his grandmother and the ones before them. About his own changing body, which is starting to look too much like his father's. He thinks about his forbidden body, his body barred from himself, devoured by history, rejected before even existing. He walks, he jumps on sidewalks, slaloms between dicks and avoids junkies sprawled out in their limbo. He reaches the boulevard, doubles back to Rue Perrinon, and crosses it once more, just to see. To rack his brain once more over his problem. He re-haunts the labyrinth of *lanvil*-downtown to pull at the last thread that still links him to reason. At the statue of Empress Joséphine, in the cool lush greenery of La Savane Park, he stops. His blood, which had boiled white-hot under the stars, takes a plunge to his ankles, bam. Kim looks upon the pearly skin and the heavy folds of the most famous of fiancées. The curves of her back, her arms, lascivious and serene, make her look like she could swoon now. "Ah! Let her fall, let her liquefy, this fucking statue! How sweet it would be to see, just once, a slaver die on a public square." As he utters those words, Kim runs his hungry eyes along the bloody line of her neck, where, long ago, someone had painstakingly sliced her head off. "This is her only judgment." He spits on the pedestal of the statue of the empress, where one can still read the dedication of her bastard husband Napoleon, and he turns around, pushing off against her. Hitting the ground, Kim flies straight to Canal Levassor, having sipped from the empress's bloody carotid the strength he needed to flesh out his idea. He, too, wants to slit history's throat, spill the blood of his memory, fell the heads of the murderers of his blood and dream of a tomorrow freed from the ceaseless trampling of their victorious bodies.

Part cries from beyond, part memories, he hears in his steps, in his mind, the words of ghosts muddled with the songs of nocturnal poets echoing everywhere in the streets of Foyal, as if they knew more than him, as if they knew better than him how to cross worlds with their lethal drugs.

The following week, the city, her diurnal words that irritate one's entrails and her nocturnal words that serenade an end-of-the-world litany. The city takes Kim's body. He always feels her muddy tongue on his skin. She troubles his sleep and drools cold sweat in his pores at dawn. The city takes Kim's breath. At dusk, she brings him the cadavers of those lost at sea, and come nighttime, she coaxes him with desires and explosions. The city takes Kim as one takes a child. When the city smiles at him, Kim wraps his arms around her. In need of an embrace, he slips between her sheets and dies with her when daylight comes.

Kim wants to get it over with. Dying wouldn't be enough. They'll have to die together, in an act of courage, to put an end to a life stretched by centuries, that never figured out how to save itself from suffering. Kim wants to put an end to the unjust litany in which each generation silences the wound that preceded it. Kim wants to put an end to the lies by plunging his lineage into eternal silence.

Kim wants to kill Cédric because it is easier to kill a child than to kill a memory. Kim wants to kill Cédric because, without that, even with Kim dead, the memory of the unpunished crime would survive.

To Make People Talk

APRIL 23, THE 10 A.M. open-line radio broadcast. The manhunt is on. People joke, the ambiance is playful, behind the radio sets. Should we talk about a woman hunt? But is it really a woman? Is it really a man? The journalists reorient. We are looking for an individual who killed a child. Well, that's true, it's an absolute scandal, but aren't we all responsible for this tragedy? A man is talking, a man of faith, a pastor in his spare time. He says: When you invite the devil to your table, he stays to eat morning and evening. We knew that sin had descended upon our land and taken root. We let the inverted enemies of Christ proliferate on our island. Now we're paying the price.

We are speaking about a person who killed a child, reminds the journalist. A feminist is on the air now. She is asked to be brief. She points out that we never insist on the gender of a criminal when it's a cisgender man. The journalist thanks her.

Abject! Horrible! A monster! A young woman is on the air. She has a thought for the mother of the child; there is no worse punishment than to lose a child, she prays for her.

A woman insists on getting on the air. Her voice is strangled. She calls upon the entire population to find the guilty one.

The journalist rattles once more the emergency number for the tip line.

No, the caller corrects: she is calling upon the people, she doesn't trust colonial justice. In prison, this child murderer, this monster, will live a few years on our dime, and then she will be freed because the jails are full. You can't trust that justice, no. You must take justice into your own hands. We must take justice into our own hands.

The communication is interrupted, the producers pulled the plug on it. The journalist and her colleague call the public back to order: We must let the police do their job, and the radio station does not condone calls for hatred, let alone murder. It's forbidden by the law. Does anyone have valuable information to share on the air? The suspect is a transgender person named Kim. He was last seen in front of his sister's house, where he was visiting with his nephew. Kim is twenty-six, 1.77 meters tall, he has black skin, shoulder-length dreadlocks, earrings, and long, fine scars on his arms. He is armed and dangerous. The victims are a six-year-old child named Cédric, and Frédéric Justille, a thirty-eight-year-old civil servant. Young Cédric was last seen on Friday at 5 P.M., as he was leaving the after-school program at Jane Lero Elementary. He was wearing the school's beige uniform. If you've seen either of these two individuals yesterday and wish to testify, call our number.

Radio silence.

The debate migrates to Telegram. People share pictures of Kim as a girl and as a boy, along with bits and pieces of the book of Genesis. No one can quite recall the victims' names. A message goes viral: "A young Afro-Caribbean transexual woman killed a child from her family this Wednesday afternoon in Dillon. Please share any information you may have concerning her whereabouts. Let's intercept her so we can put an end to such ignominious acts in our country!"

<<< >>>

The message invades WhatsApp, Facebook, Twitter. That's not good. Who published that? People don't realize that's not acceptable. The newsroom is abuzz. Not a word on the air, but the radio host who had called for order earlier shares the post on Telegram. She is tagged by a resentful colleague, and we find out in the middle of the broadcast that the star of the mic called for the murder of the murderer. After the show, she's called into the director's office. The shouting match spills out into the hallway: censure privacy dictatorship.

By noon, Martinique is on the lookout for a degenerate trans who killed a kid in the boroughs of Fort-de-France, a sinister story of narcotics and prostitution. Disgusting, but what can you expect from a deviant from Dillon, right?

An Instagram user makes a funny video where the trans fucks a child. It discreetly makes the rounds at the police station. Come on, it's just for a laugh. You gotta relax sometimes.

Chief of Police Jean-Severine smashes a service smartphone against the wall. Silence. Shock. She slams her office door. Is she on her period? People ask. Burst of laughter above legs splayed wide open.

To Erase His Face

“EVERYONE WANTS TO KILL someone now and again. It’s just that there are monsters out there who actually go all the way.”

In the *kaz*, Kim started a game of checkers with Laurent. To pass the time. “For real,” Kim confesses, “it’s not my first time. One night, already, I almost killed someone. I was exhausted, it’s true, after one of those deep post-love-making sleeps, the kind of dark hole in which you let yourself free fall. And I wanted to stay there, immobile, moist. But a bone-chilling scream woke me up. It bounced against the walls like a carnival whistle. I opened my eyes. The city light cast orange shadows in my room, apocalyptic sulfur stains that reminded me of the Parisian sky. Dreadful. I blinked to block them out, and the voice of this woman shattered my universe. Again. She was saying: *Lakay-mwen! Ban mwen lakay-mwen, bann makoumè! Ban mwen’y, mwen di zot! Zot konprann mwen pa sav ki koté zot yé? Ban mwen’y! Pè pé pé, mwen pé ké pé! Ah! Kouté sa, kouté! sakré isalop!*

“I didn’t give a shit about this crazy *Négresse*’s ode to sunrise, I was at the edge of the abyss. I grabbed the bottle of Bay Rum that was on the nightstand, and in one jump, I was across the hallway, the living room, and at the window. The nappy head of that rasta hobo was right below my window. I dropped the bottle. Poor aim. The bottle fell into the dumpster next to her. It didn't even break. The crazy woman didn't even notice. I could have killed her that day, you know. And maybe I should have. I couldn't have done what I have done if I had gone to jail for offing an old junkie *Négresse* who was drooling her life away in the streets."

That old lunatic has Maman's voice. Maybe she sounds a little bit like great-grandma Léonide. Like all the foremothers, she carries this country's history, its wounds its sounds its terrors and its grandiose beauty. When she walks through the streets below, Kim is absorbed in her trance and he returns to the *kaz* in a dream. He sees it as it was before his birth, before that of Maman and her ancestors. Kim sees children who have fallen into the dirt and been left there until they consent to their own deaths. Kim sees them scream between the hands of women overcome with spasms, stunned by their blood, their bodies, their sex, their strength, and terrified by their love.

"Another night," Kim continues, collecting pawns from the board, "I wanted to go down in the streets and wrap my arms around that crazy *Négresse*. I thought about all sorts of things I could do with her. Get a beer, give her money. Take her to social services. Bullshit. I did nothing. I just listened to her voice, which announced the end of the world. She had Maman's tenderness when she would lull me with words and close my eyes upon an ocean of lies. I would fall asleep loving her touch. I would fall asleep hating her lies. I would fall asleep, I wanted to know, to see, to touch her world. She only gave me love, but it wasn't enough. I wanted to kill her as much as I wanted to love her."

Kim wins. He puts away the pawns without savoring his victory. A spasm digs a furrow between the assassin's eyes. A grain of remorse. Kim reads the world's judgment in Laurent's eyes. He sees himself in the mirror of his cornea, a horrific criminal. And yet. Yet everything he did, he is sure of it, he did it for love.

"I didn't want the little one to suffer," Kim assures Laurent. "I was also incapable of slitting his throat. He hasn't done anything bad yet. He didn't deserve to suffer. Those eyes . . . His agonizing eyes . . . I will remember them for the rest of my life. I will regret it for my entire life. But it wasn't me! Me, I tried to kill him fast so he wouldn't suffer. I didn't want to strangle him, I wanted a gun, you know. Last week, I asked the Cuban guy on the fourth floor to find me a weapon. He threatened to call the police . . . *Tjip*, people don't live up to their reputation . . .

"I ended up killing Cédric with my bare hands. It was that or the knife. I strangled him as I looked into his eyes. He was waiting for me. Édith is never there on Saturdays. She spends her weekends in Macabou with the marabout. Frédéric had been with the little one since the previous evening, and like every Saturday, he asked me to watch his son for an hour while he took care of his business. I entered the home like one enters a naked land: as if it were mine. I found Cédric reading on the couch, already alone. He got up and ran toward me. I didn't greet my nephew, I just stretched my hands toward his throat and squeezed. He thought I was playing, just for a second. Then he quickly got it. Cédric knew he was about to die. He knew I was going to kill him. I see him I see him . . . He flails, he scratches at my forearms, I throw him against the workbench. I can't knock him out, he is bleeding. He looks at me. He looks at me . . . Right then, I think I had a doubt. I didn't want it anymore, it no longer made sense. He's just a kid and he has nothing to do with any of it, I thought. Maybe, maybe him, if we let him try to become . . . But Léonide was spurring me, and I was no longer thinking, so he closed his eyes. And in his sallow face, I recognized your hollow cheekbones, Laurent, and then mine, and this mouth, my mouth that never spoke out. I saw on his terrified face all of our cowardly silences. So I squeezed harder. And then I let go. He was dead. And then I waited, in silence, for a long time, and there wasn't a single sound in my lost mind, I waited, deciphering my wayward memory in the yellow of the walls and the flaking plastic paneling. I drank the air, a putrid mix of burnt trash nitric sand and aerosol pesticides, without a word, alone, running in my trapped mind. I waited for the one who, just yesterday, pissed the names of all the women in my country, the names of all those who die each day in silence for him to spill his treacherous semen! Frédéric came home an hour later. He opened the kitchen door. He saw his son on the floor. He didn't say a word. Stupefaction: surprise. I stuck my knife in his back. Again. And again. And I cut his head off. It wasn't as easy as I thought it would be.

"When I left, I caught a glimpse of my face in the sideboard's cold glass. I saw that fucking rapist blood entrenched by my ancestors, still there. So I left and walked walked walked and landed in a bar downtown, and I drank, I fucked at the Holy Spirit, until the end of the night. And at the end of the night, I came to you.

"Now, there is nothing left. Nothing left but me dying in a cell tomorrow, dying without a lineage, dying in a cage, alone with my history.

"I don't regret anything. I had a beautiful life up until now. If it ends tonight, that's fine. People will have to know, they will have to know I wasn't a wreck. I wasn't a junkie adrift on the sidewalk. I picked my death, more glorious. I wasn't a wreck, no. I was a flagship. I'm sure some people will get it.

"Alright, I am going to fix myself a drink. Bleed the fuck out, Laurent. We ain't got all day. Pfff, check out this colonizer's bottle you got here, aren't you ashamed of drinking this stuff with a slaver's snake tattooed on it? You're really a piece of shit. I wouldn't even touch this thing's glass. Wait, here you go. A good bottle of Neisson, that's a real drink for someone who's about to die. Ah, I feel it right here, the heart of my country, right here I feel my drum rejoice in the *fondok*-depth of my silences!"

Outside the window, in Régale, the world is singing something. Kim can't hear it. Outside, it's beautiful.

His body stretches in the shadow of the barricades he erected, he sips his rum staring into the void, his back straight, his legs spread out, his feet anchored in the cement of his territory. His knife is in his pocket. He killed someone, no, he killed three men: Cédric, Frédéric, and then Laurent. And he is going to get caught. And here is what the man has become, for lack of heroes, here is Kim embodying what he thinks is a man when in fact, he had never stopped being one.

To Honor the Wife

ELEVEN A.M. MRS. JUSTILLE REMAINED silent at the news of her husband's death. Chief of Police Jean-Severine looks for the most minute quiver of the spouse's eyebrow or lip to orient her investigation. The clock is ticking. No time to waste on commiseration. A six-year-old child and his father have been killed. The killer is still out there. He is armed.

"Mrs. Justille . . . do you know who would want to harm your husband? Or his son?"

"I don't give a damn about what happens to my husband, ma'am. And it's the first I hear of this child. So allow me to elude the question."

"Ma'am, when's the last time you saw your husband?"

"Am I being detained?"

"No, no, it's just that . . ."

"Get out of my house. Next time you want to talk, you can contact my lawyer."

The glacial glint in the woman's eye shatters the chief of police, who doesn't know what to make of it. She digs deep into her experience to help her assess the situation. Mrs. Justille does not release the grip of her eyes. She adds: "We always mourn the death of a child. But that guy was a son of a bitch. Maybe it's all right to let him die without any descendants. If you're looking for a mourner, go talk to his widow. In Macabou. And have a great day. Mine is not off to a bad start." She turns around and goes back to sit her thick body, wrapped in floral-print satin, in front of her TV screen.

"Tonight, we'll celebrate too," Kim prophesies in the *kaz*. "But that's not my thing. From now on, my thing is to no longer be someone. My thing is to no longer be from here. My thing, it's going to be four walls between which I'll drag my parasitic carcass for the rest of the century and piss everybody off. I hope that in jail, I'll be able to hear the frogs at night. I don't mind being behind bars, I wasn't good for anything on this side of the big gates anyway. But silence . . . yeah . . . that scares me. I would just love a cage with a garden view. That, and something to write so I don't go mad. And the frogs will sing for me. My mother will send them, she will tell them my name, the location of my cell, and in the middle of the night, their cry will tell me that she is thinking of me. Yeah. I believe in those things. Some people believe in God. Those are the ones we should pity."

Alcohol flows once more in Kim's muscles, and it freezes his time. He lives the last hour in slow motion, he slips into an old black-and-white film. Alcohol glides and drags the lost memory of Kim's spoiled genes. "I didn't leave my life behind, no, I see it every day, I take it in my arms like a letter forgotten on a bench, and I open it, my life, I open it! And it's all good. I spent it it's all good. Leave me here, leave me here to croak in my corner like a lost child, like nobody's child, like the forgotten child nobody ever saw. Give me water to die the death of a martyr. My belly is weary. I am sprawled out in the muck, sprawled out on the naked floor of dead sentiments. I am an insolent rag that suddenly rises like a flying carpet! Look at me, Papa! Alcohol courses through my sluggish veins and eructs its acid vapors in my sighs. I am the poet of my time, I am the one to end time! The time of somnolent dreams where my quartered life blossoms anew! Alcohol courses through my veins and I wait patiently for it to forget the silence of hard wounds earned along the way, the silence of soft words scattered in my path. Alcohol stretches the way back along my arms when I blow between my fingers. Forget me, you who know where I'm from. Forget me, who crossed your path to rip out my beloved's throat to cut the dissonant thread of my own lineage!"

To Get Revenge

"AND NOW YOU'RE LIKE A PIG on Christmas. Drained of all your blood."

Kim delights in the spectacle of his father's body, sprawled out in the living room.

There are no doors in the *kaz*. Polite people know where to stop their feet between the outside and the inside. On the doorstep, the whole world averts its eyes, diverts its feelings and judgment from the somber light emitted by the home. It's uncouth to burn one's eyes in the acid of dirty laundry. There's no door, but the wall is there. It doesn't budge.

So when Kim arrived in front of the *kaz*, at three in the morning, his feet covered in mud, pebbles, and his clothes stained with blood, the wood shamed him, forbade him passage, and ordered him to step back and wipe his dirty kicks on the doormat. Even the assassin knows to yield when the wood asks. It's so gratifying to be obedient.

Quietly, he pushed the kitchen door that opens onto the patio, the door that, according to Maman, our father never locked. Kim turned on the lights without a care; it woke Laurent up. The man got out of bed, shirtless, shocked. “Who is there?” Thick and heavy, his footsteps made the house tremble. A robber would have fled on the double. Kim stood there, stumbling, his back against the wall, waiting for Laurent to enter the living room. He didn’t let him talk. He didn’t even let him see him. He didn’t want to have to explain, anyway, there was nothing to explain. Laurent was a rapist who would never see the inside of a jail cell. Kim attacked his father from behind because he didn’t even deserve to know who was killing him, and in one swift move, he pulled his skull back by grabbing his hair and, with his free hand, slit his trachea and his carotid. It’s easier the second time. The colossus choked on the terrible gurgle of his own blood and let himself get dragged, spasms and all, to the living room couch. Kim dropped him there, and when Laurent stopped moving, Kim sliced open the veins of his ankles and wrists, sat in the rocking chair and watched him bleed out, slowly, until the end of the night, then all morning long. As he was purging that extra drink, Kim screamed at his father all the things he had always dreamed of saying. He killed time by methodically breaking every single object that adorned the living room, and he watched TV to wait some more, to wait for the body of his father to be entirely drained of its blood before pulling down his boxer briefs and slicing off his sex.

“You don’t deserve this sex,” Kim declares now. “You’re nothing but a coward, a piece of shit, who snatches the illusion of his own power by devouring the bodies of innocent girls. You don’t deserve to be called a man or even a human. I am a human. I wasn’t born with a thing dangling between my legs but I am a man. I take care of my own, even if they aren’t born of my flesh. I choose to love and I am ready to die for what I love. I am ready to kill for what I love. I am the hero Ayo, Célestine, Marie-Magdeleine, Léonide, Sidonie, Maman, and Édith should have had as their protector! And now, the snake is drained of its blood.”

Kim places the flaccid gray object in a jar.

It's over. Kim avenged me. He killed the man who raped me as a child. He killed the man who brought rape to my house. He killed the child, heir to the rape. And the blood of the criminal that soiled his lineage now flowed underground. He thinks I am purified. He thinks I am free now. He thinks I am once again the child I must have been before and whom he never knew. The child in that house hanging on the *morne*, who perhaps played dolls, perhaps rode her bike and climbed in the garden, perhaps laughed dancing around Maman. I am a child once more, by the magic of the knife, and maybe I can finally start living. Return to my home.

Kim's gaze floats over the couch and meets the window. There, far away in the frame, the *morne* basks in the glow of a new softness in the multicolored rays of the afternoon sun. There, Léonide sings him a sweet lullaby that takes his gaze over the *morne*'s curves and brings him, beyond the woods, to the forsaken corner of a hamlet, which he sees upside down. And there, on the heights, his eyes meet the freshly cleared patio of Maman's house. And his heart beats fast.

"Something is writhing, something is wiggling, can you feel it? Something is boiling somewhere. It's inflating a black and yellow ball," Léonide moans softly. Kim listens carefully: "I think it's the sun . . . Wake me up, you who know who I am. My being my blood, my childhood dream, you. Blow on my legacy so I can seize hold of it . . . the past. Spending your days gnawing at a memory will destroy you. It's like that snake embroidered on our flags, a slaver's trophy, it bites time, and it doesn't go away. The moon remembers the days when we burned the snake. Will *you* remember? Me, I don't forget. I don't forget anything. It's the injurious burden that strangles me. Come out. Come out. Come out! Come out of your bed at last. Emerge from the poison where you lie. Come out and bring to the ashes the wreckage of your nightmare. Come back to me. Burn the bitter cadaver of your legacy."

<<< >>>

Kim grabs the jar with one hand, and with the other, he brings down all the furniture that obstructs the living room. He turns his back on the putrid flesh for good. His mission is not over. The story is not over. His heart beats fast in a feverish hollow, his conscience whispers that perhaps the story will never be over. He screams without knowing what to scream and he kicks the shutters open to run across the patio and plunge into the garden.

The air, warm, the wind, ravishing. The sun. Scintillating. Beauty is everywhere under the cottony blue sky. In the human silence of the neighborhood, birds play and leaves whisper. Kim breathes. "Will you know will you know how to purify your ancestors' land? There, that's where our secret is coded. Come to me . . . Son, I will show you. Bring your trophy and call me so that I may come. And I will show you how to end the story."

And Kim takes off running, covered in blood, insolent, without so much as a last look toward the criminal's house. Kim is off to burn his mother's.

To Crush Our Silences

"WHY?"

I scream.

My ribs crush my insides and all of my organs rush to my throat, which I offer to the starry ceiling of my sanctuary. I spit the five liters of my blood, my flesh my lymph my bones my boiling bile. My tongue, dried up by the cry, writhes in pain and my distraught eyes can no longer find their orbits. I want to die. I want to cast out this strangled soul from my body, this panicked spirit, this remnant of me that lets out its last sigh before disappearing.

I urinated on my legs while sobbing on the floor. I feel for my life on the tiles, to try to put it on once more and get back up. I stumble, I lose myself. I am lost. "Get back up, Édith, we have to leave now."

I look daggers at the ghost as if it were she who had killed my son. I get out of the trance she threw me in, and I take hold once more of my words my thoughts my own being, and I can't stand anything, I no longer want to stand anything, not for one more second. My eyes roar and curse the ghost for the ignominious torture she has been inflicting upon me from the moment she set foot in my living room to prevent me from leaping at my brother and killing him. Ayo holds my gaze. She insists. "Get up and gather your things. Now, we leave."

I am collapsed on the coffee table, my blouse is soaked with tears, my hands are torn by my fingernails digging deep into my flesh. My voice gets lost in the cavernous breath of my sobs. I hold life between my hands, and life is running out like water. I melt, and with me, the citadel I built on the ruins of my eviscerated body collapses to dust on the floor. The cry has escaped, too. I no longer have strength, not even for anger. I don't even have words for the pain. My nerves are twisted in the fold of my belly. There is nothing left in my panicked throat but the childish question that obsesses me.

"You just held me here for six hours, and now you want me to follow you out? Demon!"

"I can't let you kill him. Today, he is our last heir."

"So what then? You want to initiate an assassin? My son is dead! *He* was your heir!"

My arm hurls at the ghost the bottle of poison that put me in a trance this morning, but it goes through her and explodes against a wall. Ayo stares at me, severe.

"Kim wears your wound like his own, Édith. He has been dying slowly since that morning when he first heard the dull sounds of Laurent's body pushing into your childhood sex. Kim was waiting for a word from you to avenge you, Édith. And you knew that even in the absence of a word, one day he was going to seek revenge anyway."

"No, no, Ayo. Don't you dare put my brother's quest for virility on me, you don't know him. It's that horde of sex-deprived peacocks he's been hanging out with since childhood that put a knife into his head."

"And you knew it."

"Yes! Yes, I knew! I knew, and maybe I let him. I let Kim kill the rapists, I let him! Yes! But my son, my son is innocent!"

"It's Léonide. She whispers to him everything his heart longs for. She sings revenge to him like a victory perfume. Kim is lost. Kim is ignorant. But Kim is full of certainties."

"You really want to forgive him for everything? Because you think he is your son, the one that was taken from you in 1828, you really want to believe he has no fault in this? That it's that crazy old hag who bewitched him?"

"No," Ayo retorts. "Léonide didn't bewitch him. She just convinced him."

I resist. Ayo sends me the Breaths. The Breaths lift my body, amputated still, and stretch time long enough for my blood to fall back to the floor. I get up from my trance. I understand, I assure Ayo I understand, I will follow her, and I won't kill Kim. She must stop now. My spirit can no longer take it. But my body resists still. Cédric was innocent. Cédric is a child. Cédric is only six years old. Cédric has school on Monday. Cédric promised to draw me a picture when I come home. I prepared a new remedy for Cédric's eczema. In Cédric's eyes, there is a glint of beauty that only Maman possessed when she smiled. Cédric's voice trembles on the "a" when he says Maman. Cédric runs a little bit sideways, but he runs very fast. Cédric loves his Maman. Cédric loves his father. I left Frédéric as soon as I found out he knocked up a young girl from the neighborhood one day when I was late for our rendezvous. Knocked up. More like raped. I didn't want to see him anymore. Yet I let him see his Cédric.

"But Cédric did nothing," I lament once more.

"Now get up. We must leave. God's people are already on their way to burn this place down."

"Let them!"

"For the last two years, you've broken your back moving the sanctuary here. You use your powers to redraw our vévé on the wall, but the door in Macabou is not yet complete. Now you must save the one in Régale."

"Keep a sanctuary in Régale? Where Léonide hanged herself?

Where Sidonie killed her husband? Where my mother died? Where I was raped over and over again? That house has killed enough. Let it char! I want a sanctuary that celebrates life."

"That house is also where your mother loved you. And if the vévé burns, we will all die, Kim, you, and us too, forever."

"So be it."

"Stop your nonsense, Édith. You will never have the luxury of dying. I do not give you permission. There is too much to do here. You're wrong if you think that dead spirits are the only ones responsible for the crimes of the living. I will keep my house clean in my world, and you will stay in yours to do the same, because history is not over. Hurry up. Grab the chalk in the sanctuary and do as I say. It's time to leave now."

To Reopen a Tomb

LÉONIDE'S BODY SHIVERS in the family vault at the Saint-Esprit Cemetery. I draw closer to completing the ritual imposed by my foremother. I hate her. I wish I were powerful enough to send Ayo back to that tree where large thorns pierced her body two hundred years ago. I don't dare verbalize that thought in my mind, for she would surely perceive it. I also hear in the ethers the rage named Léonide. I, too, am tempted, here in front of her casket, to answer the call of the queen of hexes. I feel that in revenge, my anger could die. And whatever devastation she unleashes upon this world, Léonide could never take more from me than Kim did.

"She could," Ayo answers. So she can hear my thoughts, the witch. "Léonide could take more from you. She could take the meaning of it all. She could take the future because anger cares very little about the future."

I cannot comprehend. I am angry. But I can no longer challenge the ancestor. I open the jar of seawater brought from Macabou, and I spill it around the vault, and I let Ayo quiet Léonide down in Yemaya's waters.

Near the *kaz*, under the kapok tree in Régale, Léonide feels the call of the rope. Already mute, she takes one last look at the fugitive body of her heroic descendant and returns to the branch she came from, in reverse, dislocating in rhythm her protruding bones. She doesn't have the time to tell him what to do with his father's sex. She doesn't have the time to help Kim avenge his own childhood. She doesn't have the time to name his mission. There, Léonide chokes on her silences.

The frogs don't understand a thing about this backward dance. But they don't do anything to stop it. Their sisters are already spreading the news of a neighborhood girl making strange libations at the cemetery to cast an evil spirit back into the earth.

In Kim's apartment in Foyal, the cops found entire notebooks explaining how and why Kim was going to kill his nephew, his brother-in-law, and his father. They think Kim's father could still be alive. But they are too late. An earthquake could not have wreaked more havoc in that house at the edge of Régale. A putrid smell wafts from the living room, where the flies are already feasting on the blood of the emasculated quinquagenarian. The team wastes no time in morbid fascination. They have to move. "Where are you, you damn fool?" hisses Chief of Police Jean-Severine, turning her gaze to the *morne.*

To Know

I AM ON MY WAY.

Kim is in front of the house. His sweat spread the blood splashed on his chest. He catches his breath. He didn't see anyone in the streets. He is certain that he is under Léonide's protection. In truth, the neighborhood is hiding away, panicked, sure that something grave is on the brink of happening.

Kim holds the jar in his hand. He is ready. He enters the garden, looks for the shed where Maman often summoned me and calls out: "Léonide! Open the way for me, show me! I want to know! I am worthy now to take my place next to you in our Pantheon!" But there is nothing in the shed. And Léonide doesn't answer. Léonide no longer answers. Kim tries to steady his heart, he closes his eyes, opens his arms, lies down on the ground, tries, with all the might his spirit adrift can muster, to connect with the world he knows exists but cannot see. The trees around him seem to crash on his body and his certainties. "Léonide! I'm here! I'm big, I'm big, I am a hero as mighty as Ayo! Léonide! Teach me her secrets I am worthy of being her son!"

Léonide is dead, but Kim doesn't know it. Ayo threw her on a bridge to a destination unknown. Ayo lifted the spells that had protected her until then. Ayo killed her descendant to save history and to try once more to build a prosperous world for her children.

"Léonide!" Kim screams loud enough to awaken the entire neighborhood. His godmother hears him, cloistered in her home, a few meters up the *morne*. She is the one who, with a trembling hand, picks up the phone in her living room and calls the police with a strangled voice.

"Léonide . . ." Kim gets up and runs through the garden. A sliver of knowledge is not enough to make a decision. A sliver of knowledge is only the appendix of true wisdom. So the dread that had been crawling at his feet now devours him through the calluses of his bloody sole. "What do I do?"

Kim puts his hands on the wooden facade of the shed in the garden. He doesn't know what to do with it. He doesn't know what to do about any of it. So his father's sex, staring at him, is no more than a hideous and morbid object that disgusts him, that embarrasses him.

Maman always waited for Kim to be asleep before bringing me to this shed. She would tell me: "I'm going to show you something." And hungry for knowledge, I would get up from the couch, docile, and put on my shoes to walk across the garden and pick medicinal plants under the bright moon, singing old lullabies whose history the grandmother would tell me when she would visit.

In the shed, small bottles of alcohol preserved the bulk of the herbs gleaned by three generations of *kimbwaseuses*-conjure women. We liked them better this way, rather than as tisanes. With Maman, the night crafted elixirs whose vapors would bring us to the gates of another world. It is in this shed that we would meet with the ancestors. I learned from them how they pushed back the gates of the living to upset death and called death sometimes to upset the living. I had to learn quickly and start early to produce abortives, remedies, spells, and to gather in my blood the wild energy accumulated by centuries of war for tomorrow's battles.

"You must keep this power, train it. One day, you will know that it's your turn and you will play your role in history."

"Maybe we will never win," I pointed out. "Maybe we will still suffer. Then would we still have to fight?"

"That's how we are still alive," Maman would answer.

Maman never hid anything from me. But she died too soon for me to find the strength to tell her what I was hiding from her. I didn't want to kill Maman. I didn't want to tell her: "Maman, your incantations were useless for me." I didn't want to hear Maman say: "In truth, we are cursed," I didn't want to hear that it was Maman's fault. It was his fault. It was Laurent's fault. It wasn't her fault, Maman, if her lover was a rapist. She would have died to have not been able to protect me. So I didn't tell Maman anything. And even at the hospital, when I would dab Maman's pearled skin with tumor-killing oils, when I made her inhale synedrella herbs to keep the pain at bay, there, on the threshold of the in-between-worlds, I was still not ready to tell Maman that our father had raped me, as a child, for years.

"You reserved this secret for me," Ayo replies to my daydreams. "Your dead mother listened to you here, crying on her remains. She listened to you, sobbing, tell the story of what Laurent did to you, but it was too late. She knew that silence would kill her children. So she wailed. And Léonide found out. And Léonide crossed over. And she talked to your brother."

Knowing did not turn me into a murderer. Knowing did not give me the desire for revenge. Knowing did not arm me. I didn't pour my poisons into the public well to assassinate all those who inherited the situation. I didn't damn an entire people even though I had the power to do so. Knowing did not make a monster out of me. Knowledge liberated me. In the mirror, looking at myself, I'd see the heroic faces of my mothers and of those men standing next to them, who shared their glory and their love. In the mirror, looking at myself, I'd see more victories than defeats, for what country celebrates its defeats? Looking at myself in the mirror, I was my own country, proud. And I grew up like that, queen of my own kingdom, of my own body, recaptured each day against oppression, against the acquired certainty that one could possess someone else. Looking at myself each day in the mirror, growing up, I'd see my foremothers, dead and living, and grateful, I would say: "I am the root of my root. I am the pillar of my single home. I am my own heroine. I am the woman of my life."

And Kim knows nothing. Kim doesn't know that each time a *kimbwaseuse* killed a child born into slavery, it was an act of love as much as it was an act of resistance. Kim doesn't know that Ayo also had a yard in her garden where she would watch over the children of the plantation and teach them how to dance. Kim doesn't know that, for the most part, children were born, lived, and that what little love grew in that awful world was given to them until the last drop. Kim doesn't know that history has transmitted more love than violence. Kim doesn't know that everywhere the flesh suffered, a caress came to soothe it. Kim doesn't understand that all the wars our mothers waged against the oppressors were to give their children, him, me, a land in which to live free at last. Kim doesn't know that, before him, before his sinister plans, before his cries, his mothers had already won by simply surviving. He doesn't know that Sidonie, his grandmother, played in this garden with Simon, our great-grandfather, when she was a child. He would take her every day to pick Julie mangos. Bassignac mangos. Maracujas. And then oranges. *Chadèque*-citruses. And the lime tree, when it bore fruit or its fragrant leaves. Simon would lay his eyes tenderly on this child, and Sidonie's hubris was her father's greatest pride. He was moved by the smallest of her achievements, refreshed even by her biggest misbehavings, impressed by the strength with which she already searched the earth for sweet potatoes and planted with him yams and *dachine*-taro. That man wasn't Sidonie's genitor, but who cared? He was her father, the man who loved Léonide despite her mental illness, and who accompanied that child, Sidonie, loyally, all throughout her existence. A true father, the kind that hugs you when your face is wet with tears, the kind that opens possibilities where the whole world says no, the kind that listens, and whose words, rare and just, trace a path for children to follow. He wasn't perfect, Simon. Who ever was? But he was there. Even after Léonide hanged herself. And that man knew how to love. The Breaths often told Édith how Sidonie would cover her father's cheek with kisses when she would come home from school. They also tell me how women, among themselves, have always carved out love to build citadels, and that's what I read in Marraine's eyes when she would speak to Maman. But Kim doesn't know any of this. Kim only knows what he wants to hear about the Breaths. The joyful days, the butterflies, the long afternoons spent cooking and gardening together are not engraved in heroes' chronicles. So Kim knows the history of the heroes, but in truth, he doesn't know History.

To Not Know

KIM BRUISES HIS IGNORANCE against the walls of Maman's house. Kim opens its doors by ripping out the shutters damaged by the last hurricane. Kim returns to the living room, the bathrooms, toppling what's left of the furniture and the cabinets in search of a passageway, a secret, a secret that is coded in his braids that was always sung to him but never revealed. He would like to ask Léonide to reveal the secret. She doesn't respond, so he sings it, he screams his oath to bring her back: "For it is in the roots of your black hair that all the power rests . . . For it is the whirlwind of your dark curls that ciphers our secret . . . For it is in the storm of your rising locks that the seal of our silence will break." But it is only a nursery rhyme in the mouth of Kim, who knows nothing.

Kim reaches the room I occupied as a child. He sees the bed its bars its used legs its tired mattress. Kim staggers. Kim forgets. Kim doesn't want to know anything anymore, Kim wants to kill again. There is no one left to kill but himself, he who said nothing, did nothing, he who let his father live for another twenty years by his silence. Himself, for being weak, for being vile, for just being, by fear, by silence, the accomplice of a rapist. He sees himself in the mirror. It's easier to kill than to kill yourself, isn't it?

Léonide is not there. No one answers. Kim can no longer stand this body that itches. Kim can no longer stand the sound of his own breathing, Kim can no longer stand the smell of this room, Kim can no longer stand the minute that just passed nor the one that is coming, for even dead, the dead is still there, even with his grandson dead, the dead is still there, even with his body, mutilated and dead, the dead is still there! His damp scent is still there on this floral-print mattress!

So Kim runs screaming to the kitchen, exhumes a bottle of alcohol from under the sink, finds a match and smashes the bottle against my bedroom wall. He strikes the sulfur, blows, and lights up a fire to burn what's left of the story.

"Stop!"

I grab Kim's arm who intends to pour in the house the bit of gasoline he found in the garage. I called the fire department. They're already on their way. A neighbor alerted them too. The police will soon be here. I have fifteen minutes. It's not enough.

"It's over Édith," Kim says, laughing through his tears, "it's over, I killed Laurent, sister of mine you no longer have anything to fear, I avenged you, I avenged our mothers!"

"You killed my son!"

"Yes, Édith, you needed me! You knew what needed to be done, but you didn't have the strength to do it, he would have been like his father, he was already like his father!"

"You know nothing! I don't need you to live! I didn't ask to be saved, I didn't ask for my son to be killed!"

"That's what they would have wanted!"

"Who?"

"Our foremothers! And you know it! You know it better than me! You see them, you speak to them, you are their heiress, you know it's our duty to kill the murderers and you did nothing! You are like that man, there, you don't do anything, each day you let a new sun rise over an atrocious world and all you do is read books, cry at white marches, sell trinkets and love potions to adrenaline-starved idiots while pretending to be an African mage! You shut yourself in a lie Édith and I sacrificed myself for you to be free!"

The slap I dealt my brother threw him to the floor. And I didn't hit hard enough.

"You, you stole my life just as much as Laurent stole my childhood! And here, you steal the lives of our mothers to dig an absurd revenge! Help me put out this fire!"

"Why? You hate this house! It's your nightmare!"

"And why do you think I'm fighting so hard to keep it, you fool? It's My life, Kim! It's My house! It's My legacy! This is where our secret is sealed, where our mothers were born, where their souls remain, where the door of the in-between-worlds stands and permits them to survive through our blood! This is where our history is, Kim! You cannot burn history, you can't erase history! That wood. Does not. Burn!"

And the fire dies.

I take it within me and I pour it into the heart of Hairun's volcano, where Ayo poured my anger. And I remain. I no longer run, I remain.

In Macabou, my sanctuary turns to ashes under hallelujahs and Christ's vengeful torches. There is nothing left of it. Ayo's vévé, which I was tracing, is but dust. In front of me, Kim's body drapes itself in mist and becomes transparent. My hands, too, are fading from the present. I can no longer hear Ayo, but I see her on the shore of the world. We are dying. My heart beats fast, ready to burst. I run into my mother's room, leaving my brother behind to dissolve into ignorance. I run, I run through the embers, in my hands, a bottle full of my blood mixed with chalk.

There, in front of our vévé, in front of the door to the in-between-worlds drawn by Léonide, that door where all the Breaths are already fading from the wall, I throw my blood on the canvas to awaken them. Far away, on the ocean, a black smoke leaves Macabou and rises to the sky.

I am alone now in the ashes of my story, my history. Outside, near the lime tree, the police are cuffing Kim and reading him his rights. I don't watch them take my brother away. In the beauty of the golden rays that glisten through the leaves of the orange trees, I search for the shred of existence that keeps me standing. My steps take me across this garden of light where worlds, times, and memories commingle, all the way to the foot of the grafted lime tree, where Kim, not knowing what else to do with it, left the jar containing his father's sex.

Translator's Notes

1. *Madou* is an Antillean beverage made with fruit tree leaves and cane sugar.

2. Foyal is another name for Fort-de-France.

3. In Kreyol, *tan Wobè* ("the Robert Era," in English) refers to a dark time in Martinican history. During World War II, France's newly minted Nazi-backed fascist government sent military contingents to Martinique, under the command of Admiral Robert. This was a period of rationing and racism.

4. Chlordecone was a carcinogenic pesticide that was shamelessly used in Guadeloupe and Martinique from 1972 to 1993, even after being banned in the US in 1973.

5. "Self-made" is in English in the original. *Poto mitan*, or the center pillar, is the quintessential metaphor used to describe Caribbean womanhood. Mother, caregiver, wife, sister, perennial cheerleader, the *poto mitan* is a selfless being devoted to man and nation. She holds the entire edifice for them. And for as long as they have been called *poto mitan*, women have rejected this role and attempted to define womanhood in new ways.

6. Slavery was first abolished in 1794, when a delegation of Haitians traveled to the Assemblée Nationale in France to point out, gently, the absurdity of declaring all men equal—as did the 1789 *Declaration of the Rights of Man and of the Citizen*—all the while keeping hundreds of thousands of Black people enslaved. Napoleon swiftly reinstated slavery in 1802 to fund his bloodthirsty wars. Slavery was finally abolished once and for all on April 27, 1848, under the Second Republic.

7. Paname is a French nickname for Paris.

8. The italic text "*happy, nappy*" is in English in the text.

9. "The marabout's wife? She has a big *kaz* at the bottom of the savanna that leads to Macabou. She has a garden, she has plums, she has limes, she has plants for all sorts of ailments, she could open a pharmacy."

10. The italic text "*beach parties*" is in English in the text.

11. La Savane Park is a popular open space in the heart of Fort-de-France. A statue of Napoleon's wife, the Empress Joséphine, was erected there in the 1850s. Decapitated in the early 1990s, it had never been restored. It was finally put out of its misery in 2020, in the wake of George Floyd's murder, which had led to a global outcry against anti-Black racism and a call to decolonize public spaces.

12. Those who run the carnival as *Nèg gwo siwo* coat every inch of their bodies in a thick black syrupy mixture that smells very sweet. This is an homage to maroons who were said to cover themselves in *gwo siwo* before escaping the plantation to camouflage themselves and get the mastiffs off their scent.

13. "You don't want to let us in. You don't want to let us in! In the Antilles, you give us water contaminated with chlordecone. You tell us in French we must obey the law? Go fuck your mother!" I translate here to highlight for the reader the spiciness of carnival slogans.

14. "Boeing, they call him Boeing. How many children does he already have here, and he needs to put another in the belly of my cousin." "She could have kept her legs shut too, though." "He didn't ask her permission. The guy didn't even ask her permission." I translate here because this dialogue contains crucial information.